Invitation to a Funeral

At twenty-eight years of age, Joseph Carver is the youngest college professor in the whole of the United States. He is estranged from his father, the sheriff of the little Kansas town of Bluff Creek. But when his father is gunned down during a bank robbery and his mother dies of grief shortly thereafter, Joseph is forced to face his family demons and return home.

He knows where his duty lies and, after his parents' funeral, he arms himself and sets off in pursuit of the men who shot his father. His quest takes him into the Indian Nations, where he receives help of the most unexpected and surprising nature.

By the same author

Fugitive Lawman

Invitation to a Funeral

Jethro Kyle

A Black Horse Western

ROBERT HALE · LONDON

© Jethro Kyle 2015
First published in Great Britain 2015

ISBN 978-0-7198-1583-6

Robert Hale Limited
Clerkenwell House
Clerkenwell Green
London EC1R 0HT

www.halebooks.com

Typeset by
Derek Doyle & Associates, Shaw Heath
Printed and bound in Great Britain by
CPI Antony Rowe, Chippenham and Eastbourne

CHAPTER 1

Will Carver knew when he woke that morning, even before he had really come to, that today was somehow special. Then remembrance struck him like a hammer-blow; this was to be the last day of his working life. It would be his sixtieth birthday in three days and today, Friday, April 4th, was when he finally quit law enforcement, after a career spanning the better part of forty years.

Rolling over in bed to cuddle Linny, he discovered that she wasn't there. Now, as he listened, Carver could hear his wife pottering around in the kitchen; presumably cooking his breakfast. Linny knew that this was an important day for him, but also one likely to be tinged with a little sadness; the end of a long chapter of his life. She was probably determined to send him off to work with a good meal inside him.

'Something smells good,' said Carver, as he entered the kitchen. 'Lord, Linny, you needn't've gone to all that trouble!' This last remark was prompted when he saw the table, a fresh linen cloth upon it, groaning under the weight of a spread such as he did not recollect ever having seen at this time of day. 'It's barely eight. What's with all this?'

'It's your last day at work, Will Carver. You didn't think for a moment that I'd let it pass unmarked? From tomorrow, you'll have plenty of time for leisurely breakfasts so you may as well start getting used to them.'

After he had gorged himself on toasted bread with honey, porridge, scrambled eggs and muffins, Carver said, 'If I eat like this too often, I'm apt to get fat and lazy.'

'You? I don't see that happening in a hurry,' said Linny. She paused for a moment, as though wanting to say something, but unsure of how it would be received. Carver knew his wife too well. He chuckled and said:

'Ah, now we come to it. I thought that breakfast was too good to be true. Trying to bribe me, ain't you? Come on, out with it! What favour are you after begging? Money for a new dress for this wretched party next week?'

'Have you written Joe and invited him for next week?'

Carver sighed. He had been expecting this question for some little while. He said, 'Joe knows where we are. He knows it's my birthday next week and what's more, I'm sure he knows we'd be glad to see him.'

'But you've not written special to ask him to come?'

'The boy knows where we are. He can get in touch if he's minded.'

'He ain't precisely a boy, you know. He'll be twenty-nine years of age this year.'

This talk about his son was threatening to cast a shadow over the morning and Carver was anxious that nothing mar this last day of his as the sheriff of Bluff Creek. He said, 'Tell you what, Linny, why don't you wire him and ask him to come. There, will that make you happy?'

His wife came up and put her arms round him. 'Thanks, Will. Oh, before I forget, I got something for you. Been making it, odd times over the last few weeks.' She opened a drawer and pulled out a bright red, woollen muffler. 'There, just the thing to keep the cold off your chest these sharp mornings.'

Carver looked at the scarf aghast. He knew he couldn't possibly wear such a thing, leastways, not till his retirement had officially begun. 'It's lovely,' he said tactfully, 'but I can't wear it to work. The fellows in the office would chaff me no end! Tell you what. Keep it safe here and I'll put it on first thing tomorrow morning.'

'And you really don't mind if I wire Joe?'

'No, you go right ahead.'

At the end of the great War between the States, there were men on both sides who couldn't quite settle down to the peace after the signing of the surrender at Appomattox Court House in 1865. Some of these restless souls took part in the Indian wars, fought for Juarez in Mexico, helping to oust the so-called 'Emperor' Maximilian, or signed up as scouts and suchlike. Some even became lawmen, while others turned bad and took up as bandits; robbing stages, trains and banks.

At the end of March, 1879, five men of this type were sitting in a bar-room in the little Kansas town of Coffey, working out where they would next be able to procure some money. This was a perennial problem for such men. Odd times, they had in their possession more money than most men might see in a year or more, but it ran through their fingers like water. If one of them had a hundred dollars one week, it was by no means uncommon for that same fellow to be cadging the price of a whiskey the next. A couple of heavy nights at the Faro table, combined with a visit or two to a cathouse and buying drinks all round in a saloon could easily wipe out such a sum within a matter of days.

The five men sitting in the Silver Horseshoe had carried out jobs together in the past. They weren't exactly what you might term a 'gang'; they had agreed to meet here and figure out some project in which they could combine to net more profit than they would make operating alone. Their names were Emile Beauregarde, Jed Sutter, Brent Flynn, Patrick Tarleton and Jack Morgan.

'Is not getting easier for boys like us,' said Beauregarde. 'Every day comes some new trouble. You hear where they hanged the Barton brothers last week? Just caught them and then strung them up at once. Pouf! All finished!'

'You're a cheerful beggar, Beauregarde, I don't think,' said Sutter. 'We all heard 'bout that. What's the use o' dwellin' on such things?'

'To make us careful,' said Beauregarde.

'Well this ain't going to get the baby a new bonnet, as my grand-papa used to say,' remarked Jack Morgan. 'Any o' you fellows got any practical schemes in mind? Or we just goin' to sit here bemoaning how hard the times have got for outlaws and such?'

It was only eleven in the morning and the Silver Horseshoe was all but deserted. The barkeep was busy, sweeping the boardwalk outside the saloon and there was only one other customer in the place; a decrepit-looking old drunk on the other side of the room.

'I got an idea that you boys might take to,' said Jed Sutter, 'but if you do, then we'll have to play it my way.'

'Settin' yourself up as a leader, Sutter?' asked Morgan. 'I don't know that any of us want such a thing.'

'I ain't asking to be a leader, nor anything like it. I'm sayin' that if the rest o' you like what I suggest, then I arrange the thing as'll be best.' Sutter looked

9

round the table at the others. He was greeted with indifferent shrugs and noncommittal grunts. 'All right then, best we forget it,' he said.

'No, let's hear about it first,' said Tarleton, who did not talk as much as some of the others. 'Tell us a little about what you have in mind and we'll see how it listens.' There were nods of agreement.

'Here's how things lie,' said Sutter. 'There's a little town about fifty miles from here. You wouldn't think it that important and you'd be right. 'Cept for one thing. It's surrounded by a whole heap of farms and there's a railroad depot too. Got one bank in the place, where a lot o' folk pay in the money they make from the stores and so on Fridays. The railroad puts money in the bank that day as well. Bank opens on Saturdays and then farmers and so on draw out money to pay wages an' stuff. Point is, Friday nights, that bank's just full of good cash money. No bonds or nonsense of that sort, just real money.'

'Where is this wonderful little town?' asked Beauregarde curiously.

'Ah, you tell me first if you're all in,' said Sutter. 'I ain't about to have some other bastard ride up there and beat me to it. You boys want in or not?'

Jack Morgan said, 'And you really ain't wanting to be a leader or aught of the kind?'

'No. I just want that if we hit that bank, I arrange the robbery in my own way. Equal shares all round and afterwards you can all get to the Devil for all I care. I don't want to be no leader of anybody.'

Morgan looked round the table. 'What do you others say?'

There were murmurs of assent and one by one, the other men said that they were agreeable to the plan. Beauregarde said again, 'So where's the town?'

'It's a little place, you boys might not've heard of it. It's called Bluff Creek.'

'I guess it's too late today to get up there and take this bank?' said Brent Flynn. 'How far away did you say it was?'

'It's fifty miles from here,' said Sutter. 'We wouldn't make it by close of business. There's no reason, though, as we shouldn't amble over that way in the next week and hit it next Friday.'

'Next Friday?' said Morgan, 'That'd be the—'

'It would be Friday, April 4th,' said Sutter.

Carver's two deputies were already in the office when he arrived. He said, 'There's no point you boys polishing apples for me, I don't get to decide whether either of you steps into my shoes next week. You know well enough the town meeting tonight'll vote on the new sheriff.'

Dave Starr and Bob Watkins looked a little crestfallen. Both men were hoping to take over Carver's job next week and ever since they had learned of his impending retirement had fallen over themselves to put on displays of efficiency and industry; plainly hoping that he would put in a good word for them before the town meeting. It was wasted effort, however, because Carver had been privately told that the job was almost certain to go to an outsider, a former deputy marshal from Kentucky. He hadn't mentioned this to them because it was pleasant to see the two young men doing their jobs properly for once.

'So what's happening today, boss?' asked Watkins. 'Me and Dave was laying odds on if you'd be in today. It bein' your last day and all.'

'I'm being paid for a day's work,' said Carver. 'You boys ought to know me well enough to know that a day's work is what I'll be doing.'

'Are we invited to this big party next week?' asked Dave Starr. 'They say everybody else is going.'

'Ah, that nonsense,' said Carver dismissively. 'That's my wife's doing. Supposed to be combined with my sixtieth birthday. Sure, you boys are welcome. Everyone else is comin', from all that I can collect.'

Everybody except my own son, thought Will Carver. The thought made him feel a little melancholy and he said to the two deputies, 'You fellows can do as you will for a spell. I'm going to take a constitutional up Main Street. Just so's folk know that I'm still on the case yet awhile.'

As he walked slowly along the street, tipping his hat and nodding to those who greeted him, Carver found his thoughts turning to Joe, his son. His wife thought that there was an estrangement between them because of Will's stubbornness and that if he would only unbend a little, then everything would be fine. If only it were that simple! He and Linny had done all that they could for their son, up to and including elocution lessons, so that he wouldn't have to speak in the same slovenly and ungrammatical way that they did themselves. They also paid for him to go to college. The result was that the boy had grown away from his own family. He felt shamed by having such plain, homely and unassuming folks, when so many others at college had parents who were hot-shots in Boston: businessmen, judges or even senators.

By the time he graduated, Joe, or Joseph as he now wished to be known, spent his vacations with friends from the Kansas State Agricultural College; fellow 'Liberal Arts' scholars, although whatever the hell 'Liberal Arts' meant, Will Carver did not to this day fully comprehend. When Joe was twenty-two, Carver had taxed him with being a snob who was ashamed of his own mother and father. The boy had made no effort to deny it and from that day onwards, Carver had made few attempts to keep in touch. Joe conde-scended to allow his mother to visit from time to time, but she let slip after these brief trips that Joe never introduced her to any of his friends. He had a professorship at the college now and was apparently doing very well for himself.

Carver was desperately anxious to keep from Linny the knowledge that her beloved son now looked down on her and despised his background. It would have broken her heart. Much better that she should believe that Will was vexed with the boy because he hadn't turned out manly enough and that the blame for any coolness did not actually lay with their son. Carver would do anything to protect Linny from the hurt of learning how matters really stood.

The day wore on, Carver occupying himself largely with paperwork, which he detested. He was damned, though, if he would allow his successor to claim that he had inherited a pigpen. By four that afternoon, he was more or less caught up with all his accounts, warrants and everything else. He thought that he would take one last walk up Main Street as sheriff and then leave his deputies to carry on running the show. It would do no harm to break the habit of a lifetime and leave work early for once. He was due to finish at five, but who would blame him for going home a half hour before that?

Fifteen minutes earlier, Jed Sutter and his four companions had been sitting on their horses, just outside Bluff Creek, and Sutter had been giving what sounded suspiciously to the others like orders for the raid on the bank; instructions which were chiefly concerned with not drawing undue attention to themselves. For all that he had denied wishing to be their leader, Sutter was surely throwing his weight around now and this had not gone unnoticed.

'We'll ride into town separate,' said Sutter. 'I do

not want us arriving in one big band like this. Morgan and Beauregarde, you go in first. Don't loiter around the bank, just ride up and down looking like normal citizens. Ten minutes later, I'll ride in with Flynn and then after a couple more minutes, Tarleton here can join us. For God's sake, try not to look like soldiers reconnoitering a position or nothing of that sort. Represent yourselves as farmers who have come to town to buy some frills and furbelows for your sweethearts and wives.'

After reminding them that the clock on a nearby church was in plain view of the building against which they were to mount an assault and that they were not to meet outside the bank until a few minutes before four, Sutter sent off the first pair.

Bluff Creek was at that time a pretty little town with many white-painted clapboard buildings and not a few others built of brick. Such a one was the imposing building which housed the offices of the First Dedham County Savings Association. It was a stout, two-storey, red-brick structure, with green wooden storm shutters. The building was topped with a triangular pediment in the classical style and both this and the surrounds of the windows and doors were painted white. It was reckoned by some citizens to be the most elegant and stylish building in the whole town.

On the ground floor of the bank was the public hall, where folk went to deposit, withdraw and sometimes borrow money, while on the floor above were the offices where the clerks worked at their accounts.

Sutter and Flynn trotted at a genteel pace along Main Street. He and the others had taken pains to tidy themselves up for this day; shaving carefully and ensuring that they looked as clean and wholesome as any other regular citizen of the town. Sutter was glad to observe that Beauregarde and Morgan had obeyed the injunction touching upon hanging round outside or in the near vicinity of the bank. Sutter could see them looking in shop windows and leading their horses sedately along the road. There was nothing that, to Sutter's practiced eye, was calculated to alarm even the most suspicious of men into apprehending that a daring robbery was about to take place.

At about the same time that Jed Sutter was entering Bluff Creek, Professor Joseph Carver was scowling with irritation at the telegram which he had just received. It read:

> JOE YOUR PA SAY AS HE WOULD LIKE TO SEE YOU AT
> HIS BIG PARTY STOP PLEASE SON PLEASE COME STOP
> HE AND ME BOTH WANT TO SEE YOU SO STOP IT IS
> MONDAY NEXT STOP LOVE YOUR MA

Professor Carver didn't know what annoyed him more about this communication; the slapdash grammar or the fact that it had been sent at all.

At twenty-eight years of age, Joseph Carver was the

youngest college professor in the whole of the United States, a fact of which he doubted his parents were even aware. He had fought tooth and nail to get to where he now was; a respected academic with tenure at the best college in the state. He did not hate his parents or anything of that sort; they were merely an embarrassment to him.

Although he lived only thirty miles from Bluff Creek, he had visited his parents no more than a half dozen times in the years since he had graduated. Each stay at his parents' house had been more awkward than the one before. His mother was so different from those of his fellow members of the faculty. For one thing, his mother and father had always refused to have servants; his mother did everything around the house, even emptying the chamber pots and sweeping the sidewalk outside the front gate. Joseph felt utterly mortified every time he saw her engaged in such menial tasks. It had got to the stage when he could not bear the very idea of staying with them. As for celebrating his father's birthday with a bunch of yokels and Lord knows who else, well it wasn't to be thought of.

Professor Carver sat back in his leather armchair and considered the most tactful way of declining this unwelcome invitation.

It lacked but a few minutes to four and so Sutter and his companion dismounted outside the bank and tied up their horses. The other men wandered up in the most casual way imaginable and began also to secure their horses to the rail. None of them spoke to each other and anybody watching might have supposed that the five men were strangers and wholly unknown one to the other.

Sutter glanced up at the clock across the street. It showed a minute to the hour. He and the men who had ridden into town with him strolled casually towards the bank.

CHAPTER 2

The hall inside the bank was cavernous and quiet, putting Sutter in mind of a church. There was a long counter at the back, behind which the cashiers were working. Sutter went over and joined the line in front of one of the cashiers. There was only one woman in front of him and she was soon finished conducting her business. It was Sutter's turn. He handed a ten dollar bill across the counter.

'I wonder now, could you oblige me with two five dollar notes for this?' he inquired politely. As the cashier fumbled in a drawer, Sutter saw that all the other men were now assembled and in their places. He pulled out his pistol and thrust it across the counter, pointing it at the man's face. One of the men who had entered the bank with him handed him a carpetbag, which Sutter pushed across the counter. 'Fill this with all the money you have. If you don't, you and your friends are all as good as dead.'

Morgan, Beauregarde and Flynn had moved to the

counter and having withdrawn sawn-off scatterguns from their long coats, were now aiming these in the general direction of the other cashiers. The fellow to whom Sutter had spoken didn't seem to get the idea too quickly. He just stood there gaping. '*All* the money?' he asked, bemused. 'I don't rightly understand you, sir. I thought that you had requested two fives for a ten?' His bewilderment was obviously real; the idea of a bank robbery in daylight hours just didn't seem to make sense to him.

'Fill the bag with all the money you have, or before God I will shoot you down right now,' said Sutter quietly. The man seemed then to grasp the notion, because he began throwing bundles of notes and sheaves of papers into the capacious bag.

'I'm sorry,' the cashier said after a minute of this, 'but I don't think it will all fit in this here bag.'

'You must have bags back there,' said Sutter. 'Fill those as well.'

'Yes, sir.' said the cashier.

Flynn had, as agreed, moved to the street door and as people entered, was shepherding them to a corner and covering them with his gun.

'I think that's about it,' said the cashier. 'We have some bearer bonds; do you want them as well?'

'No, you can leave those,' said Sutter. 'Just hand over those bags of cash now to my friends here.'

The other three cashiers collected the full canvas bags and passed them across the counter to Sutter's men. When they had finished, there were three large sacks and the carpetbag to carry out. Sutter and the others gathered themselves together and he gave both the cashiers and customers to understand that the first person to leave the bank or raise the alarm after he and his men had departed, would be shot down without mercy.

Everybody was feeling right pleased that the whole enterprise had gone so smoothly. The five of them left the premises of the First Savings Association of Dedham County with smiles on their faces and songs in their hearts. All that remained was to mount their horses and hightail it out of there. It was at this point that things took a wrong turn.

Now what Sutter and his boys couldn't have known was that there was a foot pedal behind that bank counter, which connected to a wire running up to the offices on the first floor; something after the fashion of a bell-pull. This was so that if ever a cashier was not sure about a cheque or was doubtful about the identity of an individual attempting to make a withdrawal, all that was needed was to jiggle that pedal, which sounded a bell in the upstairs office. Then either the manager or one of the clerks could come down and see what was what.

On this occasion, the pedal had been operated not once but twenty times. A clerk had come down, opened the door to the main hall, seen that a robbery was taking place and then retreated upstairs again quietly without being seen. The manager of the bank, a man called William Staunton had been alerted. As chance would have it, Staunton was going hunting that weekend and had brought his rifle with him to the office, so that the moment the bank closed, he could travel straight to his friend's farm.

Jed Sutter knew nothing of all this. He and the other men had just finished transferring the contents of the canvas sacks that they had brought out of the bank into the leather bags hanging over the front of their saddles, when there was the rattle of a window being thrown up overhead and a voice cried:

'Throw down your weapons!'

They looked up and saw William Staunton leaning out of the window, pointing a rifle at them. Now, whatever else you could say about Sutter, he was a bold and decisive man, never hesitating to take swift and deadly action when he saw the need. On this occasion his first instinct was to pull his pistol and begin shooting at Staunton, who at once commenced to return fire.

Flynn, who was standing next to Sutter, fell dead; half his head blown away by a heavy calibre bullet from Staunton's rifle. Tarleton, Morgan and Beauregarde were now directing a withering fire into the first floor windows of the bank. Sutter was seized by a killing rage and pulled his own rifle from the leather scabbard at the front of the saddle. In the meantime, Staunton had vanished from view, either shot or staging what is sometimes known as a strategic withdrawal. Sutter fired at the windows of the bank, first those on the first floor and then the lower ones. His men did likewise, until there was not a whole window left in the part of the bank facing on to the street.

'Bastard!' exclaimed Sutter. 'Murdering bastard son of a bitch.'

'Jed, we better make tracks,' said Jack Morgan, 'Anybody could've heard all that.'

Somebody had indeed heard the shooting. Will Carver had heard what sounded like a gun battle breaking out ahead of him. He couldn't see what was happening, but people were diving for cover at the other end of Main Street. He began running in that direction to see what the heck was going on. By the time he reached the bank, the shooting had ceased and he saw four men mounting up; evidently with a view to riding off. Carver drew his pistol and shouted, 'Hold up, you men. Don't any of you make a move, now.'

Even now, after hearing the shooting and seeing the smashed windows of the bank, Carver could not quite believe that such a thing as this should be happening in his own town. He confidently expected the men he had hailed, to dismount and explain their conduct to him. His main emotion when Sutter shot him twice in the chest was not fear but bewilderment. He fell to the dusty road and died and even in death, his face bore a look of surprise that somebody should have shot him.

As for the men who had raided the bank, they went down Main Street in a thunder of hoofs, sending passers-by scurrying out of the way. Before most of the citizens of Bluff Creek were even aware of what had happened, the men who had robbed their bank and murdered their sheriff were already heading south towards the Indian Territories.

Linda Carver was just taking the cake from the oven, when there was a rap at the front door. Had she been a little less genteel and well-bred, she might have uttered a curse word at this point, but as it was, she limited herself to saying, 'Oh, darn.' The Carvers lived right on the edge of town; far enough from Main Street that Linda hadn't heard the shooting. When she went to the door, it was to find Will's deputy, Bob Watkins, standing there, with Dr McPherson.

'Hallo, Bob,' she said. 'What brings you out here?'

The young man seemed to be tongue-tied and unable to speak, which was unusual for him. He generally had too much to say, as Will had often remarked to her privately.

'Whatever ails you, son?' asked Linda Carver. 'You been struck dumb or what?' She said all this in a playful manner, smiling so that Bob Watkins would know that she was only joshing. She noticed that Dr McPherson had a grave look upon his face and suddenly felt alarmed. 'What's going on?' she said.

'Linda,' said Dr McPherson, 'let's go inside. I got some news to give you.'

'What is it? It's not about Will?' She saw from their

faces that it did indeed concern her husband and she said sharply, 'Just tell me right now. What's happened?'

'Will, he went for a walk. Some men were taking the bank and he ran into them,' said Bob Watkins and Linda saw, to her amazement, that the young man's eyes were filling with tears.

'Where is he now?' she demanded. 'Doctor, tell me straight, where's my husband?'

There seemed no point in dissembling and Dr McPherson laid his hand on her shoulder and said, 'He was shot, Linda. He's been killed.'

Her first impulse was to deny that it was so and to cry that it wasn't true; that her husband would be back home directly. But deep inside, Linda knew that it *was* true. She began screaming aloud, 'Oh God, no, no.' With some difficulty, the two men managed to get her inside the house and persuaded her to sit down on the settee in the front parlour. Linda continued to shriek and wail, while Bob Watkins and the doctor looked at each other, neither sure what to do next.

Joseph Carver was pleased with the telegram which he had composed in reply to his mother's invitation. He did not actually commit himself to going to his father's birthday party, but nor, on the other hand, did he say that he would not be going. He had written on the form:

DEAR MOTHER HOPE FATHER HAS HAPPY BIRTHDAY
STOP WILL BE OUT OF STATE SATURDAY AND SUNDAY
BUT SHOULD BE BACK MONDAY STOP JOSEPH

The bit about being out of the state for the next
couple of days was an absolute falsehood, but served
both to emphasize how busy he was and also lay the
ground for his not being able to attend this wretched
party, about which his mother had already written
him, of course.

Professor Carver could imagine nothing worse
than being trapped at his parents' house for several
days and being compelled to socialize with their
friends and neighbours. Nothing on the face of
God's earth would induce him to travel to Bluff
Creek for such an event.

Joseph Carver had inherited a good many of his
father's characteristics; he had far more in common
with his father than he did his mother. There was a
time, when he had been fourteen or fifteen, perhaps,
when he and his father got on well enough. Those
were the days when Will Carver had somehow persuaded himself that his son had a hankering to take
after him and go into law enforcement. Nothing had
ever been further from the boy's mind. Even in those
days, he had known that there must be more to life
than that little town.

While he and his father got on reasonably well, the
old man had taught him to shoot, something for
which young Joe proved to have an aptitude. Fact

was, as his father boasted proudly to his friends, Joe was a better shot than he himself. But it had been ten years now since Joseph Carver had so much as picked up a gun. His life now was wholly bound up with books and papers and the idea of going out into the woods and shooting a jackrabbit or squirrel would seem bizarre to the man he had become.

As he strode to the telegraph office with the message to his mother clasped in his hand, Joseph Carver looked every inch the academic he now was. He was a tall, ascetic-looking young man, with steel-rimmed eyeglasses and a face permanently fixed in a look of scholarly contemplation. Already, he was becoming something of a fixture on the college campus and the older members of the faculty were saying that young Carver had a glittering career ahead of him. Professor at twenty-eight; why, it was unheard of!

Having sent his answer humming south along the wires, Joseph Carver felt as though a weight had been lifted from his shoulders. Every time he faced the prospect of meeting his mother or visiting his home town, he was oppressed by a sense of gloom and despair. He had a secret nightmare that he would one day be compelled to give up all that he had here and return to live in Bluff Creek. This was the fear which had driven him on, ever since he had started at college ten years ago. It was the defining motive in his entire life; the desire to finally be rid of his past and to reach a time when he could utterly forget

Bluff Creek and all who dwelled there.

Unfortunately for Professor Carver, events in the town which he so detested were already conspiring to draw him back to his childhood home. His worst nightmare was about to become reality and before the week was out, it was his life here in the groves of academe which would become the distant dream.

The booty from the raid on the bank exceeded the wildest expectations of Jed Sutter and his three companions, consisting as it did of a total of nine thousand, five hundred and eighty-nine dollars in cash. The clerks at the bank had diligently piled every last dollar in the safe into their bags and each of the four men had accordingly reaped a reward of just under two thousand dollars. It was vastly more than any of them had dared hope.

'God almighty,' exclaimed Jack Morgan. 'I never seed so much money in one place in the whole course of my life!'

'It's surely a welcome sight,' said Beauregarde. 'We're all running a little low lately, is it not so?'

'You might say so,' said Tarleton. 'I ain't had so much as I could o' wished in the last week.'

'Here's the way of it,' said Jed Sutter. 'I'll tell you boys how we're goin' to play it.'

'Will you, though?' said Morgan in surprise, 'It's been noticed, Sutter, that you been talking mighty like a fellow as thinks he's in charge. That ain't how the land lies at all, so you best drop all that now.'

'I only meant...' began Sutter, before Beauregarde cut in smoothly and interrupted him.

'Yes, we all know what you meant, friend Sutter,' said the swarthy little Creole. 'We work it out well enough. You mean that you'll set up as our leader. You needn't think it, not for one single moment.'

Sutter looked at each man's face in turn and all three of them met his eyes unflinchingly. The message could not have been clearer; if he did not drop all this bombast and abandon his pretensions at leadership, then the three of them might lay him in his grave. Jed Sutter was many things, but he wasn't a fool. He knew that his play had failed and that he'd better back right off and become just one of four equals again. 'Hell,' he said jovially, 'I didn't mean nothin' by it. Lordy, you fellows don't need to take on so. I ain't about to set myself above you as a leader, you got it all wrong.'

The four bandits had ridden the moon from the sky, not stopping until they had crossed the line into the Indian Nations. Technically, they were no longer under the jurisdiction of Kansas now and it would be an illegal act for a posse to ride down on them and seize them. They knew only too well, though, that the Indians were seldom able to defend their territorial integrity and that if a bunch of lawmen or even private individuals from Kansas caught up with them, they would be unceremoniously dragged back across the line into Kansas. That was if they were lucky. A posse of town'sfolk from Bluff Creek would be more likely to string them all up from the nearest tree right there on the spot. They none of them had any illusions about the fierce hostility that could be aroused by the killing of men known and respected in a little town. Their fellow citizens could be worse than a bunch of Apaches on the warpath when it came to exacting vengeance.

The aim now was to ride deep into the Indian Territories and then lay low for a space, until the bank robbery and its associated killings faded somewhat from the memory of those in Kansas. Then, the four of them could emerge in another territory and go their own separate ways. They none of them had any particular liking for each other and, truth to tell, would all be happy to part from their fellows when the time was ripe. The only one who felt some faint stirrings of regret about the notion of breaking company was Jed Sutter. For a week or so, he had almost been able to persuade himself that he was the leader of a gang of outlaws; a foolish conceit that had now been rudely shattered by the supposed members of this 'gang'.

Dr McPherson was very worried about Mrs Carver. She had been in a state of nervous collapse now for over twenty-four hours and he was beginning to think that the shock she had received had done her some mischief. Various neighbours were staying at her house in relays, ensuring that the poor woman was never alone, but to the doctor's eye, there was something more to the case than just the natural reaction of a grief-stricken woman.

'Tell me, Mr Starr,' said McPherson to one of the dead man's deputies, 'do you know about next of kin and so on?'

'Is it as bad as that, sir?'

'I very much fear so. What about that son of theirs? You know how to contact him?'

'He's teaching college, not too far from here. I guess we could wire the college and get them to pass on a message. We already sent him notice that way about his pa's demise. But is it life and death with poor Linny?'

'We'll see. If it's as I suspect and she's had a fit of cerebral apoplexy, then she might yet recover. I can't say.'

'I'll go back to the office and get that wire sent to her son. Mind, he ain't been seen near nor by for more than two years now. I don't know if he'll come.'

'Send the wire. It's all you can do.'

That Saturday night, though, Linda Carver had a seizure a little before midnight. The woman sitting up with her sent for the doctor, but it was to no avail. By the time he arrived, it was to find that Will Carver's widow was failing fast and there was nothing he could do except administer a few drops of laudanum to the almost insensible woman.

'Is she Catholic?' asked McPherson in a low voice. 'If so, now would be a good time to send for a priest.'

Mrs Barton, one of Linny Carver's oldest friends

and neighbours, was a mite put out at the notion that her old acquaintance might have followed such a heathenish and superstitious denomination as the Roman Church. 'Catholic, nothing,' she said shortly. 'She's Presbyterian, same as all the other folks in this here town.'

'No offence meant, I'm sure,' said the doctor. 'Well, whatever is needful for a dying woman in the way of spiritual consolation, that's what she'd better have now.'

'Dying? Linny really not going to pull through, Doctor?'

'No, I doubt she has more than an hour of life left to her.'

'Well then, you'd best off and tend to those as you *can* help,' said Mrs Barton stoutly. 'I reckon as I can tend to her needs as well as any parson. I'll read a verse or two from the Good Book and that might be a comfort to her.'

So it came about that Professor Joseph Carver received no fewer than three telegrams in quick succession: one informing him of his father's death, the second warning him that his mother was gravely ill and the third telling him that his other parent was also dead.

No matter what age you are and whatever your relations might be with your mother and father, it cannot be other than a shock to learn that both have died within the space of little more than a day.

Despite the fact that he had seen little of them over the last few years, Joseph Carver was still a little numbed by the news of their death. And in addition to the muted, although very real, grief, he was also overwhelmed with another and far more disagreeable emotion; that of guilt.

He may have been an academic, but Professor Carver was also a practical man and he knew that the sovereign remedy for guilt lies in action to assuage that guilt. Already, he knew that his father had been murdered and he guessed, correctly, that his mother's death was a direct consequence of her own husband's sudden departure from this world. Would it make him feel any better about neglecting and snubbing those folks over the last decade or so, if he were able to take some steps to bring their killers to justice? Carver decided that it might very well be the case. As he packed for the railroad journey south to Bluff Creek, the professor already had at the back of his mind the idea that he might look into this matter a little closely when he arrived back in his home town. If nothing else, it would keep him busy there and provide a ready-made excuse for not spending over-much time in the company of all those dullards and witless clods with whom he had grown up.

CHAPTER 3

Sutter, Morgan, Beauregarde and Tarleton were not having too good a time of it in the territories. For one thing, you could never really relax when you were in those parts. The advantage of hiding out there, that you seldom encountered the official law, was also, coincidentally and ironically, the great disadvantage of the place. It meant that you might be bushwhacked or killed and nobody would even bother to look into the matter. It was for this reason that the four of them stayed together. They might none of them be great friends, but at least a group of four heavily armed men was less likely to be ambushed and robbed than single travellers.

Federal marshals had a theoretical authority to hunt down fugitives hiding out in the Indian Nations, but none of them thought it in the slightest degree probable that the little affair of the bank in Bluff Creek was going to be treated as a federal crime. It was now three days since the murders and robbery and they had seen no indication of being pursued by a posse. In all probability, they were now home and dry, although it would make sense for them to wait another two weeks or so before they made their way into Arkansas or Texas.

Scattered through the territories were old and abandoned huts and soddies; the former habitations of white men who had taken it into their heads to come and live here, away from their fellow men. Morgan had told the others that he knew of a couple of such places, just a few miles across the line from Kansas and so when they were sure that there was no posse on their tail, the men headed east towards the foothills of the Ozarks. Sure enough, they found a deserted shack, with a roof that might just about keep out the rain. There was no door; the leather hinges had long ago rotted away and the door itself been used for firewood. Still and all, it would be better than sleeping under the stars for the next fourteen nights or so. With luck, they could stay holed up here peacefully; always assuming, of course, that they didn't get cabin fever and end up killing one another.

The town looked just precisely as he had remembered it; small, dull and lacking in anything that would make a fellow wish to spend his whole life here.

Joseph Carver stepped down from the carriage and surveyed the depot with displeasure. Lord, didn't anything *ever* change around this town? The place hadn't had a lick of paint since the end of the war from all that he was able to collect from looking at it. Everywhere he looked, there was that lifeless and worn-out feel to the place. So very different from vibrant towns like Wichita or Topeka. Well, he'd have to make the best of it. What a mercy that he didn't plan on staying more than a day or two; until the funerals were over, that was to say.

Professor Carver dropped by the sheriff's office, to find that Bob Watkins, who he recalled meeting briefly a few years ago, appeared to be in charge.

'They cancelled that there town meeting,' explained Watkins, 'out o' respect for your pa, you see. So for now, me and Dave is in charge.'

My 'pa', thought Carver disdainfully. Yes, that's just what these fellows would call somebody's father. He had not heard the word 'pa' used for years, other than in a mocking and ironic way by those with whom he now associated. Your 'pa' indeed. Carver said, 'I wonder if you have the keys to my parents' house here?'

'Why yes, that we do,' said Watkins. 'Your ma and pa are over at the undertaker's, if you'd be wanting to give your respects. I can show you the way, if'n you'd like?'

'It's kind, but I recollect where the undertaker's is situated. But I'm obliged to you, all the same.'

'Oh, that's right. Grew up round here, didn't you? Place changed much since then?'

'Not so that you'd notice, no,' said Professor Carver sourly. After he'd been given the keys, he set off to the edge of town.

The house seemed more poky and cramped than ever he could remember it being. Everywhere he moved, Carver found himself brushing against furnishings or banging into tables and chairs. It was all so different from the spacious apartments and houses in which he generally found himself these days. These thoughts made him feel guilty again. Imagine coming home for a funeral, and of his own parents yet, and then criticizing their home as being too small! He was once again consumed with that familiar irritation that he had known for years, wherever his mother and father were concerned.

After he'd got the range going, and what a dirty smelly performance that was, Professor Carver brewed up some coffee. It had been years since he'd had to build a fire in a cooking range with his own hands. That's what servants were for. When he had finished the first cup of coffee, he took out the ring of keys and looked for the one that fitted the stout closet in his father's workshop. He had been absolutely prohibited from meddling with this closet or even going near it when it was open, when he had been growing up. It was where his father kept his guns.

The locks were new and freshly oiled. Where firearms were concerned, his father had never taken any chances. It brought back a lot of memories to look inside that closet. When he'd been growing up, there had been cap and ball revolvers and muzzle-loading weapons; now, it was all up-to-date breach loaders, which took brass cartridges. Although it had been years since he'd handled a gun, Carver felt a curious pleasure in hefting a pistol in his hand and smelling the fragrance of the oil upon it.

There was an imperious rapping on the kitchen door, which Carver chose to ignore. The banging grew louder and eventually, he realized that he would have to see who it was. He laid down the Remington, which he had been examining, and went to see who was there. His heart sank, when he recognized his mother's best friend, Mrs Barton. Nevertheless, he would have to let her in, for she had seen him now.

'Mrs Barton, it's been a while . . .' he began, before the woman cut in with the greatest irascibility.

'A shade over two years since you've favoured us with your presence in this town.'

'As long as that? Time flies.'

'Your poor mother used to talk of you a good deal. She never could work out why you stopped coming to visit.'

'Won't you come in and sit down,' said Carver. 'There's coffee on the stove if you'd care for a cup.'

'Well, I wouldn't mind,' said Mrs Barton, ungraciously. 'I won't deny I could do with a rest.'

When they were seated at the kitchen table, Carver said, 'Tell me now, what efforts were made to catch the men who shot my father?'

'They sent out a posse. Headed up by those two boys as worked for him. I tell you now, nigh on every man in town volunteered to ride after those men. Your pa was that popular with folk hereabouts.'

'But there was no sign of them?'

'If there were, those boys didn't spot it. They'd vanished.'

Carver thought for a bit and then said, 'Anybody got any ideas on where they went?' He knew that Mrs Barton acted as an exchange for all the gossip in Bluff Creek. Nothing escaped her and pumping her in this way would be more likely to yield information than any number of conversations with that dolt down at his father's office.

'The Indian Nations,' she said promptly. 'That's it, for a bet. Hiding out there among all them heathen savages.'

Having found out what he wanted to know, Professor Carver thought that it would do no harm to spend a little time on the social niceties. He said, 'I'm sure it's a grief to you, the loss of my mother, I mean.'

The old woman looked at him sharply and said, 'Ought to be a grief to you, but your eyes look dry enough.'

'We don't all show our sorrow in the same way,' he said tactfully. 'I understand that the funeral is fixed for Wednesday morning?'

'That it is. You'll be holding some sort of gathering here, I reckon?'

'It could be so.'

When he'd finally managed to rid himself of his mother's best friend, Carver went back to the work-room and looked through his father's collection of guns once more. He selected a Remington .44 and a

Winchester rifle. Then he broke open boxes of shells for both weapons and filled his jacket pockets with the brass cartridges.

It was lucky that his parents' house was on the very outskirts of the town, because it meant that the professor would not have to walk through the streets carrying a rifle in one hand and a pistol in the other, which might have given him an odd character with any who saw him. He was dressed in the most respectable way imaginable and looked like any other well-heeled professional type. For a man in such clothes to be toting two guns would certainly have raised eyebrows.

It took Carver a half hour to tramp into the hills that surrounded Bluff Creek. The sound of his shooting would still be audible in town, but it was far from uncommon for men to hunt up in these hills and he was confident that the noise would not be liable to alarm anybody. He found a likely spot, just before the forest began and out of view of the town below.

Taking off his jacket and hanging it from a low branch, Professor Carver worked the action of the Winchester a couple of times, dry-firing it to get a feel for the piece. It was smooth as silk. He delved into the pocket of his jacket and extracted a half dozen shells, which he fed into the tubular magazine, somehow figuring out instinctively how to work the mechanism.

When the rifle was loaded, Carver looked round for a suitable target. A little silver birch stood maybe twenty-five yards away. He cocked the piece, sighted down the barrel and fired; all in one fluid movement. The first bullet went wide and he realized that the calibre was smaller than he had been accustomed to when he used to shoot with his father all those years ago. He'd over-compensated for the kick. Carver worked another round into the breech and tried again. This time, he hit the tree right on one side; to the left. That had always been a fault of his. He fired again and the bullet smacked into the trunk of the birch; plumb-bang in the centre, at about the height of a man's chest.

After half an hour of shooting, Professor Carver was reassured that he had lost none of his proficiency with firearms. He was sure that he would be more than a match for anybody he came up against, although he was well aware that there was more to tracking down fugitives from justice than just giving a display of fancy marksmanship. His father had told him many times that it wasn't always the man who was the best shot who came out on top in a real shooting match; it was the one who did not hesitate to fire when he was drawing down on a fellow being. Will Carver had been the first to admit that he was no great shakes as far as target shooting went. What he lacked in accuracy, though, he made up for in determination.

Already, Joseph Carver was feeling a whole lot better, purely and simply by virtue of having taken a little exercise and been shooting again. Odd, the guilt that had been bedevilling him was already beginning to fade a little. Perhaps when he caught up with the men who had killed his father and precipitated the premature death of his mother, it would vanish entirely.

When four men who do not especially like each other are cooped up in a little hut in the middle of nowhere for days on end, then one of two things is likely to happen. Either they will make a conscious decision to see how best they might rub along or their dislike for each other will begin to fester like an abscess, resulting in suppressed anger and ungovernable passions which threaten to break out at any moment.

None of the men in that little shack were very agreeable or sociable individuals. All of them were used to spending good long periods of their lives travelling alone and tending to their own affairs. This was why being in that shack was like sitting on a powder-keg getting ready to blow.

Beauregarde, who fancied himself as somewhat of a dandy, was irked at what he saw as the unhygienic habits of the other three. He expressed his views most forcibly on this subject the morning that Joseph Carver had arrived in Bluff Creek.

'You men are a filthy bunch of devils, you know that?' he asked rhetorically. 'You and you,' he continued, pointing at Sutter and Morgan, 'the two of you make water up the side of this hut, last night. I hear you doing it. I should be glad, perhaps, that you went outside to do it. But in or out, it is foul. Could you not go a little way into the woods?'

Jed Sutter snorted derisively. 'You're too delicate for this sort of life, Beauregarde,' he said mockingly. 'Happen you'd do better setting up as a Sunday school teacher or some such.'

The Creole stared at Sutter for a moment and then said, 'You follow that line a little further, my friend, and see where it lands you.'

'That a threat?' said Sutter, his eyes narrowing.

'No,' said Beauregarde, 'it's an invitation.'

'Why, you little runt . . .' began Sutter, making as though to get to his feet.

'Come on,' said Tarleton, 'let's break it up. This rate, we're like to be shooting each other directly and where's the profit in that?'

This was only the first of a series of increasingly acrimonious confrontations between the four men. They tried going for walks and taking it in turns to go off and buy provisions from the Indians, but the atmosphere was steadily deteriorating. Unless something happened to unify them, it was plain to Tarleton at least, that there would soon be murder done.

When he returned from his little bit of shooting practice, Professor Carver went straight back to the house to divest himself of the weaponry. He had it in mind to take a turn around town later that day and did not wish to look like an armed marauder.

After he had washed and shaved, Carver headed

into the centre of town to find something to eat. He didn't like being in this one-horse little town with all its memories of his childhood, but the shooting had invigorated him and he felt able to look round the place a little and see what, if anything, might have changed in the two or three years since last he had been here.

There was a little eating house at one end of Main Street, which seemed to Carver like it had been there forever; certainly since he was a small child. The interior did not suggest to him that it had been redecorated since that time either. The ceiling was dark brown from the cigarette smoke, which formed a permanent fug in the place. Carver, who was not a smoker, felt a little dizzy from all the smoke, but he doubted that it would be any better in another establishment. He ordered a plate of sausage, eggs and beans and retreated to a vacant table. Once he was sitting down, he looked at the plate of food with mild distaste. It was certainly not the kind of fare that he was used to in the college refectory.

He had no sooner begun to eat, than he observed with dismay that Bob Watkins was coming over to join him. He smiled faintly and greeted the deputy.

'Mr Watkins. Good to see you again.'

'Hey there. All right if I join you?'

'Sure, you go right ahead.'

Once he had settled into his seat and begun tucking into his food, Watkins said, 'Hear you went out armed this afternoon. What were you about, hunting?'

'Not exactly.' Carver had forgotten that nothing at all passed unremarked in a small town like Bluff Creek. Watkins had probably known about his leaving the house with a rifle before he'd even got up into the hills. How very different it was in a large city, where a man could walk all day and lose himself, with no prying eyes or inquisitive neighbours to mark where he went or what he was doing.

'Your pa, he has, I mean had, quite a stock of guns. You use one of his rifles or what?'

'Is this an interrogation? You think I'm up to no good?'

'Lord, no,' said the deputy, horrified at the construction which had been placed upon his words. 'I'm just making conversation is all. I don't mean nothin' by it. Nothin' at all.'

'I was only kidding,' said Carver. 'I know you were just chatting. But tell me, may I ask you about my father's murder?'

'You go right ahead, sir. You got every right to know.'

It took Bob Watkins fifteen minutes to outline the circumstances of Sheriff Carver's death and the consequences for his wife. The young man looked genuinely affected by the events he recited.

'And what about the men who carried out this robbery?' asked Carver. 'Is anything known about them?'

'Not a damned, I mean blessed, thing. We raised a posse, went huntin' after 'em, but there was no trace.'

'I heard they might be hiding out across the line in the Indian Nations. Is that what you think?'

'They certainly headed south. It's like as not that's where they fetched up.'

'What about the man who was killed by the manager at the bank? You find anything out about him?'

Watkins shook his head. 'He stopped a large calibre bullet right smack in the middle of his face. There weren't nothing to identify him, no papers on his body or anything.'

'You got descriptions of others, though? From the bank clerks and so on, I mean?'

'Yes sir,' said Watkins, 'and if'n you'd care to step across the way, I can let you have copies of the wanted bills we're havin' run up.'

'I'd be vastly obliged to you, Mr Watkins.'

The young deputy was looking at Professor Carver with a look of wonder upon his not overly bright countenance. 'Why are you looking at me in that strange way, might I ask?' said Carver.

'Sorry, it's just that you sure do talk different from your pa! I wouldn't o' guessed the two o' you was kin, I swear to God!'

'You're not the first person to make that observation,' said Carver drily.

CHAPTER 4

The day of the funeral dawned bright and clear, for which Professor Carver was thankful. Funerals were miserable enough affairs at the best of times and at least the sunshine made them a little less gloomy. He dressed with care, the black suit he was wearing being eminently suitable for such a sober occasion. He had already had a maid sew on a black armband before starting for Bluff Creek.

While Joseph Carver was shaving and getting ready to attend his parents' funeral, the men responsible for the two deaths were dealing with a difficulty that had arisen. The part of the territories where they were hiding out was in the Cherokee Nation. They had taken it in turns to trade at a largish settlement a few miles away, where they had been able to purchase milk, meat, cornpone and so on. It was meagre enough fare, but probably the best that they were likely to see for the time being. They had evidently excited the curiosity of some of the Cherokee, because when the first of them woke up on Tuesday morning, who happened to be Beauregarde, he found that three young men were snooping round outside their hut.

Beauregarde was invariably courteous and polite, which sometimes caused others to mistake him for being a bit of a sissy or a weakling. When he heard the men prowling round outside the hut early that morning, he stood up and walked outside at once to wish them a good morning. He automatically gave a half bow as he spoke to them, which caused all three of the Cherokees to eye the little man with amusement. They began imitating his bow and walking up and down in a burlesque of his mincing gait.

Beauregarde watched all this impassively. He was not in the habit of allowing others to take liberties regarding his manners or appearance and so after he had established to his own satisfaction that he was actually being mocked and insulted, he drew his pistol and said, softly, 'You men don't stop all that nonsense I'm going to put a bullet in somebody.'

Maybe none of the three young men understood English or perhaps it was that he spoke in such a quiet and unassuming way that there didn't seem to be any danger, but his words only had the effect of urging them on to further imitations of him. In Beauregarde's defence, it might be mentioned that he was very short tempered in the mornings and the lack of any sanitary arrangements in his present accommodation was beginning to drive him crazy. The first the other three men in his party, all of whom were still sound asleep, knew of things was that they were woken up by the sound of a pistol shot near at hand.

They armed themselves and came tumbling precipitately out of the dilapidated shack to find Beauregarde covering three Indians with his gun. One of the Indians had apparently been shot in the leg, because his thigh was running with blood.

'Beauregarde, you mad bastard,' said Sutter. 'What've you done?'

'I'm teaching manners to these savages,' replied the Creole calmly. 'I warned them what would happen if they did not mend their ways.'

'Cryin' out loud,' exclaimed Morgan, 'they probably didn't understand you. You didn't have to shoot them. Sometimes I reckon as you belong in the insane asylum.'

'They stopped mocking me, at any rate,' said Beauregard with satisfaction.

It was true that the young Cherokees were no longer impersonating Beauregarde. Instead, two of them were trying desperately to staunch the flow of blood from the wound in their friend's leg. They kept darting venomous looks at the white men. They weren't armed themselves, but it wasn't hard to see that those boys were fixing to go straight back to their settlement and gather up some friends with a view to returning and wreaking vengeance on the men who had injured their friend.

There was no point in recriminations, although Sutter, Morgan and Tarleton were all three of them furiously angry with the little Creole. There was obviously but one thing to be done and that was to dig up and leave the area without any delay.

The funeral of his parents was much as one would expect such a melancholy occasion to be. Professor Carver was not much of a one for churches these days; attending services only often enough at college to prevent any suspicion of atheism being attached to him, which would have been disastrous professionally. He had allowed Mrs Barton to turn over his parents' house into something which Carver thought resembled a shelter for the indigent and homeless, whereby those mourning his parents could drop by and have a drink and maybe something to eat. It was, he privately thought, a barbarous custom, akin to the Celtic wake.

An elderly man came up to Carver as he was standing there awkwardly, accepting the condolences of people he hardly knew. 'Your pa will be sorely missed,' this man said. 'I was his friend these last ten years or so. Just about remember you. Moved to this town round the time that you were going off to college. You might recollect me; my name is Powers, Grant Powers.'

'You must forgive me. I don't think that I remember meeting you.'

his graduation. He was reluctantly compelled to admit that he still detested his own background.

Various people came up to Professor Carver as he strolled along the street, offering their condolences on his sad loss and congratulations on the actions which he had lately undertaken. Neither were particularly pleasing to him. The morning wore away in this fashion, until it was finally time for him to leave.

When he returned to the college, it was noticed immediately by his colleagues that his leave of absence had affected some sort of change in him. It was nothing that anybody could put their finger on, just that he was indefinably different. Even the Dean remarked that if he hadn't known better, he would have supposed that rather than attending a funeral, young Carver had just come back from a health cure or some kind of invigorating vacation.

Most men carry their backgrounds around with them like luggage: the experiences of their childhood, the type of people that their mothers and fathers were and a dozen other things. Listen carefully and you can discern where they were born and raised; look closely at their way of dressing and conducting themselves and you may be able to hazard a shrewd guess as to their origins. For the last ten years, Joseph Carver had been keenly aware of this and had often felt burdened with an early life that he wished to shed. In effect, that was precisely what had happened during his trip to Bluff Creek to attend the funeral of his parents; he had enabled himself to

159

break free of his own past.

In the course of a little more than a week, the professor had lost both his parents and as a direct consequence of the actions he had subsequently taken, he had succeeded in ridding himself once and for all of the creeping sense of shame and guilt which had been accumulating over the last decade or so. He was free.

'No matter,' said Powers. 'I was sorry that the posse didn't catch up with those sons of . . . I mean those scoundrels who killed your father. Went haring off without stopping to even think about it. I tried to counsel 'em, but would they listen?'

'What do you mean, sir?'

'They just saddled up and rode south as fast as could be, without a thought. They'd o' done a sight better to ride north, but would they listen? Would they, heck.'

'I'm sorry, Mr Powers,' said Professor Carver, 'you'll most likely think me awfully slow, but why should anybody have ridden north? I understood that it was generally agreed that those men would have been heading south for the Indian Nations?'

'Sure they were. And how was anybody going to find them there? Anybody from this town speak Cherokee or Choctaw? Any expert trackers in that posse? How could they expect to hunt those fellows down?'

Patiently, Carver said, 'I still don't understand why they should have gone north, in the opposite direction from which you think that the killers rode.'

'Lord a mercy,' said the old man, letting out a loud guffaw which attracted scandalized looks from others in the parlour. 'If I ain't left out the whole entire point. Happen I'm gettin' old, son. What I'm driving at is that a couple o' miles north of this town lives old Billy Two Shoes. Old Cherokee, lived alone out there like a hermit for Lord knows how many years. They'd o' done better to ride off and see Billy. He was a good friend of your pa's, you know. He would have helped track down those boys, trust me.'

'Billy Two Shoes? Surely he isn't still around? He was an old man when I was a boy. I recall my father taking me to visit him. Used to live in a wigwam or wikiup or whatever you call it.'

'That's the fellow. Still there. He was the best tracker ever. He helped your pa out a few times.'

'So why didn't anybody run out to fetch him?'

'That young fellow, Bob Watkins, the deputy, he wouldn't have it. He was that fired up that he got everybody running round like headless chickens and just riding out without thinking about things first. No wonder they come back empty handed.'

A few more people drifted up and condoled with the Professor on his sad loss. He couldn't help but notice that some of those who spoke to him so had a reproachful air, like they secretly thought that he'd been neglecting his mother and father over the years.

'So how does Billy Two Shoes get by now? What does he live on?'

'He's set up as a Holy Man. Indians come from miles away to ask his advice and get themselves blessed. Tells fortunes too, from what I hear. Not just Cherokees either. Even hear where some white folk been up to his wigwam begging for his help. Everybody leaves him gifts of money and food. He seems to get by just fine.'

'You think he'd talk to me, if I went up to see him?'

Grant Powers laughed. 'I'm sure he would, if you took him a little present. You know where he is?'

'Yes, if he hasn't moved, I can find my way there easily enough.'

'He ain't moved these twenty-five years.'

'You are one stupid cow's son, Beauregarde, you know that?' said Jed Sutter venomously. 'What in the hell did you do for to shoot that boy?'

'He was making fun of me,' said Beauregarde simply. 'Small men have to be more careful than others about such things. If not, then they become the butt of every passing fool.'

The four men had lit out of the area just as soon as the three Cherokees had left. You didn't need to understand a word of their language to know that the youths had been saying words to the effect of: 'Wait till we come back with our friends; you'll all wish you'd never been born!'

They alternated trotting with spells of cantering. There was no telling how determined the other men at that settlement might be in pursuing them. It would do no harm at all to put as much distance between them and anybody who might be seeking vengeance as possible.

After a brief discussion, they had chosen to ride west, rather than heading deeper into the territories in the direction of the Choctaw Nation.

'I want to give those Choctaw a wide berth,' said

Sutter and Morgan agreed. The other two were happy to go along with what was decided, having no real preference either way. As they trotted for a while, Tarleton said:

'Any of you men know of another shelter we might use?'

'We had a perfectly good shelter until some fool started raising Cain,' said Morgan, glancing point-edly at Beauregarde. 'I know of a little place along this way. It's not a hut, though. It's a cave.'

'Jesus Christ,' said Tarleton, 'has it come to that? We goin' to be hiding in a cave like bears or wolves. I never looked for that to happen.'

Morgan reined in and turned to confront Tarleton. 'You want to strike out on your own, you go right ahead. I tell you now, I've had about enough of all three of you.'

'Best we stay together, though,' said Beauregarde. 'There's safety in numbers or so they say.'

'Why don't you shut up?' was all that Morgan had to say to this.

It was more common these days for Joseph Carver to travel in a horse-drawn buggy or railroad car than it was to find himself on horseback. Still, he could ride well enough when the occasion demanded. The owner of the livery stable had been disposed to discuss old times and remind Carver of the things he got up to when he was fourteen. Lord, thought Carver, after he finally managed to get away, does nothing ever change in this damned town? Fifteen years later and the same man running the stable. In the cities that he spent most of his time in now, businesses like that changed hands a dozen times a year.

The piebald gelding seemed a steady and reliable creature and it was a fine day for riding out into the countryside. Bluff Creek nestled in the midst of a patchwork quilt of little farms. It was beyond the last of these that Billy Two Shoes evidently still lived. Carver saw the wigwam, which in other parts of the country they knew as a wikiup, and halted the horse for a moment. He wanted to gather his thoughts and try to figure out the best way of presenting the case to the old Indian. The wigwam lay a half mile off the road and so he dismounted and led his horse towards it. As he approached the strange, domed structure of branches, thatch and twigs, a grave and dignified figure emerged from the low door and stood watching him.

'I have been waiting for you,' said the old Indian, in a voice which belied his wrinkled and shrivelled face. It could have been the voice of a man of forty, hale and vigorous.

'Waiting for me?' said Carver. 'I don't rightly understand you, sir.'

'You're a messenger. You have come to take me on the long journey.'

'Long journey? Well, I thought you might come with me into the territories and track down the men who killed my father. He was a friend of yours, was he not? Will Carver?'

'Will Carver? Yes. An old friend.'

Carver wondered if the old man was going to invite him into his wigwam or what the correct etiquette for such meetings might be. Would they simply stand here and talk or was it customary to sit on the ground. Then there was the 'gift' he had brought for Billy Two Shoes; twenty dollars in gold. When should he offer that?

The Indian looked to Carver as though he knew very well what was going through his mind. Billy Two Shoes said, 'Come here tomorrow. You must bring me a horse, I cannot walk far these days.'

'You mean you'll do it? You'll help me find those men?'

'Yes. Come tomorrow.'

Fumbling a little, Professor Carver took the two gold pieces from his jacket pocket and offered them to the Indian, who looked faintly amused. He said, 'Where I am going, there will be no need for gold. I am going to the tents of my forefathers soon. Keep your money; you have more need of it than I do.' Then, without bidding Carver farewell, he turned and went back into the wigwam.

As he rode back to town, Carver examined the business from every possible angle. Had the old man really known that he was coming today? It was hard to see how that could be; he hadn't even thought of such a thing until speaking to Grant Powers after the funeral, what, four hours ago? And what was all this about the tents of his forefathers?

One thing stood out, though, and that was that Billy Two Shoes had definitely agreed to go with him as his guide to the Indian Nations. It didn't look to Carver as though the old man would be much use in a rough-house, so he would have to deal with any shooting himself. Whatever would the fellows in the faculty at college have made of all this? He had already told the college that he would be gone for a week for the funeral, but it seemed to him that it would be prudent now to wire and ask for some compassionate leave; a fortnight or three weeks, perhaps.

When he returned the piebald to the livery stable, Carver engaged to hire it for three weeks from the next day. He also asked about another horse. The man looked at him curiously, saying, 'What's afoot? You taking some lady friend on a vacation?'

'Hardly that. This is for an elderly man. He's very light.'

'Got a little Indian pony out in the corral. Might suit an elderly party. Quiet as you like, you could let a child of five ride him.'

'That will do nicely, thank you. I shall want to hire tack as well.'

The owner of the livery stable gouged Professor Carver unmercifully for the horses, seeing in a well-spoken man dressed so respectably a good source of income. It was plain to him that Will Carver's boy had done all right for himself and could probably afford to pay top whack for any services. Who the elderly person might be that this snot-nosed young fellow might be going off with for a couple of weeks, he could not guess.

When he got back to his parents' house, Carver thought that he had best get himself ready for this little expedition. One thing that he had noticed was that the more action he took to avenge his parents' deaths the more the guilt he felt about giving them the cold shoulder for all those years was evaporating. It would be interesting to discuss this with a doctor some time; it had the air of a pathological emotional reaction. Still, whatever the explanation, the activity was making him feel better about things and was also serving a useful purpose as far as he could see.

It was strange to be rooting about in his parents' bedroom. Even as a child, this was the one room in the house which had been more or less off limits to him. He figured, though, that since the house and everything in it now belonged to him, then he had more right than anybody else in the world to be here.

In the ashtray by the bed was his father's pipe. The room was scented with the tobacco he smoked and the smell of it evoked memories for Carver. He went across to the window and opened it, so that the faint scent would be dispersed by the evening air. What he chiefly needed were some clothes suitable for a week or two in the saddle; he could hardly ride the range wearing the outfit he currently had on. Carver looked in the closets and selected some of his father's clothes. They might be a little tight, he was taller than his father had been – but they would have to do. He put them on and was pleasantly surprised to find how well they fitted him.

After he had sorted out some clothes, the professor went downstairs to his father's workshop and ferreted about until he unearthed an old holster and belt. He also came across a sling for the Winchester. He buckled on the belt and then unlocked the gun closet and took out the Remington that he had been practising with. It was odd to be carrying a gun in this way, although his father had encouraged him to do so when they went shooting; maybe fifteen years back. He then fitted the sling on to the Winchester and adjusted it so that he could wear the rifle slung over his back.

Having kitted himself in this way, Professor Carver went into the front parlour, where there was a pier-glass. He looked at the unfamiliar reflection staring back at him. It was a man clad in rough work clothes, with a gun at his hip and a rifle slung over his shoulder. Lord, he thought to himself, I wonder what the fellows at college would make of me now?

There were still a few bits and pieces that he would need, but that could wait until tomorrow morning. Carver thought that he might be best advised to have an early night. Unless he missed his guess, it would be some little while before he slept in a bed again and he really should make the most of it. He would be starting early the next day. The only thing he would need to do in town was to send a wire to the college; apart from that, he could just load up his gear and be off.

So it was that Professor Joseph Carver, the youngest college professor in the entire United States, armed himself to the teeth and prepared to set out after his father's murderers. He lay down his head that night soon after it became dark and slept like a baby until dawn the next day.

CHAPTER 5

The sky was overcast when Carver awoke and it looked to him as though there might be the promise of rain before the day was out. He felt anxious, not so much for his own sake as at the thought of that ancient old fellow who would be accompanying him to the Indian Nations. I can put up with a little damp and discomfort, thought Carver, but a cold on his chest and that old fellow will like as not go down with the pneumonia or some such.

When all was said and done, Professor Carver thought that he did have some responsibility for Billy Two Shoes. After all, he had asked the man for help and invited him to join in this trip south. It would be a terrible thing if the old man were to take ill and die as a consequence. Thinking about the old man dying put Carver in mind of the strange things that Billy Two Shoes had said yesterday. What the devil had he meant by talking about the 'long journey' and going to the tents of his forefathers? Was he already sick and wishing to breathe his last in the Cherokee homeland? That was a thought.

The more he thought matters over, the more the professor decided that he had better talk seriously to the old Indian before they set off south. True, the fellow was about Carver's only hope of tracking down the men he was hunting, but it would still be the hell of a thing if he dragged the old man off on a snipe hunt which resulted in his death.

After a substantial breakfast, Carver collected together canteens, saddle-bags and a few other things that might be needed. He packed oilskins for both him and the Indian and also a spare change of clothing for himself. Then he went to the gun closet, where he had locked away his guns the night before and retrieved them. He took out a couple of boxes of shells for both the pistol and rifle and then looked round the workshop to see if there was anything else that might come in handy. He couldn't see anything.

Just as he was closing up the closet, Carver noticed a little wooden keg, tucked away almost out of sight at the back. It was a five-pound cask of fine-grain black powder. Wrapped around it were a couple of yards of fuse. Nobody used black powder much for anything these days. Some older weapons used it, but it was going out of use now even for things like blasting. Most everybody these days was using nitroglycerine rather than powder. Well, you never knew what might come in useful. He wrapped the keg and fuse in oilcloth and then went back into the

62

parlour and found a box of Lucifers to put with it.

Professor Carver felt most horribly conspicuous as he walked into town to collect the horses and send the telegram. Inevitably, the first person he saw after leaving the house was old Mrs Barton, who was fooling around with the hedge in her garden.

'Lordy, but you're up right early,' she said as she caught sight of Carver. Then her jaw dropped when she got a better look at him. 'Going on a hunting trip, are you?'

'Something of the sort,' replied Carver evasively. 'I hope to be back in a week or two.'

'That your father's clothes you have on there?' she inquired disapprovingly.

'It could be so,' replied Carver. 'Well ma'am, much as I'd love to stop and chat, I have to be about my affairs. I hope to see you soon.' As he walked off, Professor Carver could feel the old woman's eyes boring into his back.

The telegraph office wasn't yet open and so Carver was compelled to walk up and down Main Street for a while, where he was the object of general remark and the theme of conversation between all those who observed him. He was uneasily aware of this, but quite unable to see how he could make himself any less conspicuous. The pistol might possibly have passed unnoticed, but the rifle slung over his shoulder did give him a dangerous and martial aspect.

It was a great relief when the office opened and Professor Carver was able to wire the college to warn them of his extended absence. Having done so, he went straight off to the livery stable and was pleased to find it open. The owner said, 'I guess you'll be wanting to collect those two mounts?'

'That's about the strength of it. Are they ready?'

'That they are.'

'Well then,' said Carver, 'I reckon that I might as well be off.'

There was a slight detour to be made before riding off to collect Billy Two Shoes. Carver had left the saddle bags and provisions at his parents' house and it was necessary to ride back there to collect them.

Living in a cave was about as low as any of the four men on the run from the killing in Bluff Creek had ever thought to sink. Staying in a run-down old cabin was one thing. You could kid yourself that it was like the days of the pioneers or even similar to Walden Pond. The prospect of spending two weeks in a cave was something else again. It made them feel like wild beasts. Beauregarde realized most keenly the indignity of moving into the cave. Even worse was where some animals had evidently been using the cave as their lair. There were heaps of dried dung scattered about and a musty, dead smell lingered in the place.

'To think,' said the Creole, 'that I, Emile Beauregarde, should be reduced to this! Living like a beast of the fields in the abandoned lair of wild animals. It is not to be endured.'

'Just stow it, Beauregarde,' growled Sutter, who of

the other three men had least patience for these airs and graces. 'It's just as bad for all of us.'

'Ah no,' said Beauregarde smoothly, 'Not at least for you, Sutter. I grew up on a plantation, with all that I could require. For me, this is a terrible come-down. A man like you, though, you have lived like this for most of your life. I dare say that you grew up in such a place. Nothing would surprise me less than to learn that you were born in a cave.'

Jed Sutter turned and faced the little man, his eyes glittering dangerously. 'I said stow it, Beauregarde. I won't say it again. Leave my life out of this.'

Tarleton tried to smooth things over by saying, 'Still and all, this ain't how any of us was raised. I can't say I take to holing up here better than the next man.'

Morgan interpreted these complaints as being a personal criticism of himself, since he was the one who had led the others to the cave. He said, 'There's nobody needs to stay here 'less they want to. I didn't march you all in here at bayonet-point.'

It was becoming increasingly clear to all four of the men that there would be trouble if they were cooped up together for much longer. Beauregarde was unpopular among them all for causing them to have to leave the hut they had been staying in and the other three all had a grudge against him. The prospect of spending much longer in each other's company was an appalling one and the fact that it was now beginning to rain made matters worse. It meant that they would be stuck here together for at least the next few hours.

Billy Two Shoes was standing next to the charred and blackened remains of his wigwam when Professor Carver arrived to collect him.

'Good Lord,' Carver said, when he saw that the wigwam had burned up. 'You weren't hurt, I hope. What happened?'

'I burned it,' said the Indian calmly. 'I will have no more need for it.'

'What happens when we come back from the territories? I only hope to be there for a week or two.'

'I will not be coming back here.'

'You mean that you will be settling with your own people, going back to live with the other Cherokee?'

'No.'

Carver had lived for so long among men who talked smoothly and argued their case fluently and with great coherence that he found blunt statements of this sort hard to comprehend. The old man did not appear to have any desire to explain himself, either to Carver or anybody else. It was positively unnatural. It was exactly the same when they had mounted up and were heading back towards Bluff Creek. The old man was seemingly quite content to ride alongside Carver without speaking a word; he was utterly self-contained.

The shortest route south was to ride into town and then go straight down Main Street, which ran from north to south, and then to carry on along the road which headed into the Indian Nations. The thought of trotting down Main Street tricked out like this in his father's clothes, carrying two deadly weapons and accompanied by the old Indian, made Professor Carver blanche. He thought about asking Billy Two Shoes if he would mind terribly if they were to go skirt round Main Street and pass through the town via some little streets and alley-ways. He was afraid, though, that the Indian might think that he was ashamed to be seen in his company; which was not at all the case.

The singularly ill-matched pair certainly attracted their fair share of attention as they trotted past the stores. Passers-by stopped to stare in amazement at old Will Carver's stuck-up son, armed to the teeth and riding along with that old Indian Medicine Man, who had been living in his shack up by the side of the road for as long as anybody could remember. One or two of the men guessed where this little expedition might be heading and thought the better of Carver for it. Showed that in spite of living his fancy life away at college all those years, he was still his father's son.

After they had left the town behind, Billy Two Shoes said, 'The place has not changed.'

'I've been saying much the same thing to myself ever since I got back,' replied Carver. 'All the changes in the world outside seem to have left Bluff Creek untouched. It's a strange thing.'

Those were the last words that the two men

exchanged for the next hour or two. Gradually, Carver became used to the notion of being in the company of somebody and not having to fill up the silence with a lot of foolish and unnecessary words. It was kind of relaxing when once you got used to it.

When they had been travelling in this way for somewhat more than an hour, and the sky was looking darker and darker with rain clouds, a thought struck Carver.

'I see you haven't brought any blankets or other clothes with you, sir. I'm not sure how we'll manage if those clouds open up, as looks probable.'

'I burnt everything,' said Billy Two Shoes, 'but I did not have a blanket anyway. I never had but one set of clothes.'

'No blanket or extra clothes? You were living out there a long time. What happened in winter?'

'I got cold and wet.' said the Indian frankly.

The ill feeling between Emile Beauregarde and the other three men sheltering in the cave erupted after they had been stuck there for the whole morning, while a torrential storm raged outside. They didn't even have so much as a deck of cards to while away the time and so the four of them just sat there, staring out at the rain, talking in desultory fashion and wishing that they could get back to civilization. The Creole began telling a long story about the plantation he had been raised on, which Sutter and Morgan chose to regard as being fanciful in the extreme.

'Come off it, Beauregarde,' said Morgan, 'you're like the rest of us, grew up without a pot to piss in. Stop putting on airs, it don't suit you.'

'You say that I was raised in a pigpen like you, Morgan? Indeed not. The Beauregardes were highly thought of in Savannah.'

'Like as not, your mother was some bar-room floozie! You're not a whit better than any of us. Highly thought of in Savannah. . . . You save those tales for girls you're hoping to screw; they don't impress us none, let me tell you.'

Beauregarde, who had been lounging against a boulder, with his chin resting in his hand in what looked to the others like a sissified pose more suited to a woman than any real man, looked up and his body stiffened. 'What was that about my mother? I didn't catch it.' His voice was soft and deadly, altogether lacking the usual languid and half-mocking tone which he habitually adopted when talking to the others. It was clear to them all that he was getting riled.

'Don't take on so,' said Sutter in a soothing tone, as though he were trying to smooth things over between Morgan and Beauregarde. 'I never knew my own father. I shouldn't wonder if we're not all of us bastards here.'

This remark caused Morgan and Tarleton to guffaw with laughter, but it was not well received by Beauregarde, who got slowly to his feet. He said, 'You may say what you will about me, but none of you say anything further of my family. I warn you all.'

Even now, under normal circumstances, things might have calmed down again, without blood being spilled. But then circumstances were far from normal. For one thing, the other three men in that cave were already vexed with Beauregarde for setting them on the run just because he couldn't take a little joshing from a bunch of savages. Added to that, they were now stuck in a cave, with no prospect of the weather changing that day and no place near where they might be able to acquire any more provisions. They had been nicely situated before, with that Cherokee settlement just down the way a bit. All of this, they laid at Beauregarde's door and now, here he was putting on side about his damned family.

Morgan also stood up, in an ostentatiously casual manner, and said, 'You're a touchy devil, Beaueregarde, which is why we're all sitting here with little food to sustain us. You might be hot shit when you're up against unarmed boys like those Cherokee, but don't push yourself too far with me. I tell you now, I won't have it for a moment.'

'You take back what you say about my mother and we can all sit down again and take our ease. You going to do this?'

'No,' said Morgan deliberately, 'I don't believe that I am.'

'Tarleton,' said the Creole, keeping his eyes fixed on Morgan, 'you want to count to three?'

'Come on, man,' said Tarleton, horrified at the

speed with which things were turning bad, 'There ain't no call for this. Why don't you fellows shake hands and forget about it. Happen the rain will clear up directly and we can go huntin' or something.'

'Count to three,' repeated Beauregarde, staring at Morgan as though measuring him up for a coffin.

Morgan said, 'Go on, Tarleton. I don't mind obliging this little weasel, if he's that set on dying. Count to three.'

Tarleton shook his head sadly. This wasn't the first time he'd seen such things and he surely didn't want to piss off either Morgan or Beauregarde by an outright refusal. He said, 'Well, if you boys are determined. You both ready?'

Morgan and Beauregarde certainly looked as though they were ready. The two men stood facing each other at the mouth of the cave, no more than twenty feet apart. They were silhouetted against the opening, with the lashing rain and flickering lightning providing a backdrop as dramatic as you could hope for, for such a life or death contest.

'One,' said Tarleton. Morgan faced the other man without any sign of fear, merely staring at the little Creole with a slight smile playing around his lips. He truly gave the impression of a man enjoying himself. As for Beauregarde, he was coldly furious. With all the devout Catholic's respect and adoration for mothers in general and his own in particular, Morgan could hardly have hit upon an insult more likely to provoke the man to violence.

'Two.' Both Beauregarde and Morgan were absolutely motionless, the whole attention of each fixed upon the other. Time stood still; they both waited for the word 'Three'. It never came. Just as Tarleton was drawing breath, preparing to initiate the duello between the two men, there came the dull boom of a rifle; the shot magnifying and echoing within the confines of the cave.

Tarleton was baffled by the turn that events had taken, as he watched Beauregarde fall to the ground. Then he realized what had happened. Sutter, sitting in the gloomy shadows at the back of the cave, had taken up his rifle and shot the Creole before he had had a chance to draw. Sutter stood up and walked over to where Beauregarde was panting his last breath, his eyes already glazing over. Jed Sutter aimed a careless kick at the side of the prone man's head and muttered, 'Little whore's son.'

'You men planned that!' said Tarleton in amazement. 'It weren't a fair fight from beginning to finish.'

'Wouldn't say exactly as we actually *planned* it, would you, Morgan?'

'I shouldn't put it so, no,' said the other man. 'But you got to allow, Tarleton, that that little bastard was getting on all our nerves to no small extent. I reckon you're as glad to see the back of him as we are.'

This was perfectly true and Tarleton had been getting as sick of the Creole's boasting and fancy ways as the other two. 'Still and all,' he said, 'that was kind of a scurvy trick to play on the fellow.'

'Well, it can't be helped now in this world,' said Morgan practically. 'He's dead.'

At about the time that Emile Beauregarde was breathing his last, Professor Carver and his companion met another traveller on the road. The storm hadn't yet reached them, although there was the distant rumble of thunder from the south. Coming towards them from that same direction was a lone rider. As this person drew nigh to them, Carver saw that it was an Indian. He was no ethologist and could not tell at a glance to which tribe the man belonged. As this rider came closer, he slipped off his horse and continued towards them on foot. To Carver's astonishment, when he reached the two of them, this tough-looking young man went up to Billy Two Shoes, dropped to his knees in the road by Billy Two Shoes' pony and then grasped the old man's sandaled foot and kissed it.

The closest comparison that Carver could think of to this action was when he had witnessed a monk meeting a cardinal some years ago. It was the same procedure, with the monk dropping to his knees and kissing the hem of the cardinal's robes. He watched, intrigued, to see what next would happen.

Billy Two Shoes good humouredly encouraged the young man to rise and addressed a few words to him. There followed a great torrent of speech from the other Indian. He still seemed in awe of the older man, but was clearly eager to tell him about something or other. This went on for a quarter hour or so, with almost all the words being spoken by the younger man and Billy Two Shoes only interjecting from time to time, perhaps in order to clarify some point or other.

At length, the flow of words faltered and stopped. The old man placed his hand on the younger man's head and spoke a few words, which the professor took to be a blessing of some sort. Then the other man mounted up and went on his way.

It would have seemed vulgar to ask immediately what it had all been about and Carver guessed that if any of it had any reference to their quest, then Billy Two Shoes would, in the fullness of time, share the information with him. So it proved, because ten minutes after they had parted from the other Indian, Billy Two Shoes said, 'You have not asked what my brother wanted of me.'

'That man was your brother?' asked Carver in surprise.

'All men are my brothers.'

There was silence for a space and then Professor Carver said, 'Does that mean you are going to tell me what was said?'

'Not all,' said the old man. 'Some was what you might term news or gossip from my tribe. But something was said that you will want to know. Four white men were hiding out near a village. When some of the young men went to see what they were doing, one man shot a Cherokee. The men in the village are hot for chasing these men and chopping them.'

'Chopping? Oh, you mean killing.'

'Yes. We must not lose time, if you want to take these men yourself.'

They carried on in silence. Carver thought about what Billy Two Shoes had said about him wanting to 'take' the men himself. It was only now, when his journey was well advanced, that Professor Carver gave serious thought to what he *did* want. Setting up this expedition and preparing everything had acted as a sovereign remedy against the crippling guilt that he had been racked with since hearing of his parents' death. The whole adventure had acted on him like a regular tonic. But now that he was actually approaching the Indian Nations where, it appeared from all that he was able to apprehend, his father's killers were hiding out, Carver supposed that he ought to decide what he was going to do if and when he found them. This is a false position for a respectable academic to be placed in and no mistake, he thought to himself: Whatever was I thinking of?

CHAPTER 6

The sudden explosion of violence which had claimed the life of Emile Beauregarde had taken Patrick Tarleton by surprise. He hadn't liked the fellow any more than the other two men, he guessed, but still and all, that was the hell of a thing to happen. It was not the first time that he had seen a quarrel between two outlaws turn ugly and result in death; far from it. It was more that he had completely misread the situation and not picked up on the circumstances which led to the murder.

Until Beauregarde had been killed, Tarleton had believed that Jack Morgan and Jed Sutter were at daggers drawn and tussling for power. Now, it appeared that there was some deeper understanding between those two that he had not been aware of. This was troubling. Having seen the ruthless way in which they had goaded the Creole into challenging a fight and then killed him, Tarleton had a not unnatural apprehension that he might end up being served in the same way. Not that either of the men had shown any signs of hostility towards him. Quite the opposite, in fact, because almost their first act, as soon as Beauregarde had stopped breathing, was to rifle through his belongings and share out his money from the bank into three equal parts. Tarleton had exhibited a little superstitious reluctance at taking the money of a dead man so soon after his death, but Morgan had insisted.

The rain had begun to ease off almost immediately after the brief gunfight, if something so one-sided and swiftly concluded could be described so, and it looked like the day might be set fine.

The storm came sweeping up from the south and caught Professor Carver and his Indian guide before they crossed the line into the territories. Carver ferreted around in his saddle-bag and found the oilskins which he had packed. Billy Two Shoes declined to share them and so Carver pulled them on over his clothes. The downpour was uncomfortable enough, even so. What it must have felt like for the old man, who was clad in light buckskin pants and a leather jerkin, the professor could not imagine.

There was no shelter to be found thereabouts form the weather; the plain stretched ahead of them with no trees under which to wait out the worst of the rain and certainly no buildings to be seen. Billy Two Shoes hardly seemed to notice the water streaming down his body and saturating his clothing.

Mercifully, they only caught the outer edge of the rain clouds which had produced the prolonged storm to the south west and the heaviest of the rain was over in little more than an hour.

'Don't you feel the cold?' asked Carver, slightly irritated by the phlegmatic way that the Indian endured the wind and rain. The old man looked faintly surprised by the question.

'I feel the cold just the same as you,' he said.

'Then why not at least take some steps to keep yourself warm and dry?'

Billy Two Shoes said nothing for a while and then, when Carver thought that he was going to ignore the question, said, 'First you get cold and put on your coat. Then soon, you are hot and take off your shirt. All the time, you are fleeing from the world. When it is cold, I let myself be cold. When it is hot, I take that too. Better than being dead.'

Well, thought Carver, that is either great wisdom or a lot of foolishness. I'm strongly inclined to the latter view.

Darkness overtook the two of them soon after they had left Kansas and entered the Cherokee Nation. So far, Carver hadn't asked the old man how they were going to proceed, but as the twilight darkened around them, he said, 'Tell me, sir, what are our plans?'

'We sleep soon.'

'And in the morning?'

'There is a village not far from here. They can tell

us what we need to know.'

The two of them pulled off the road and rode over to a little stand of trees which Carver hoped might provide them with some cover should it start raining again during the night. He tethered the horses and then unpacked his blanket. Because the old man had nothing with him, the professor felt duty-bound to offer him the use of the blanket. Billy Two Shoes refused courteously. 'I sleep as I am,' he said and positioned himself sitting upright and leaning against a tree.

As he drifted off to sleep, which took some considerable time, due to the great discomfort and alarming novelty of sleeping on the ground outdoors, Carver thought about the old Indian. Had he really had a supernatural revelation about his approaching death? Was it possible that he really did have powers that were not granted to the more materialistic white folk? It might be thought that musing about such nonsense was a harmless enough activity, if a little foolish, but surprisingly, it was nearly the death of the youngest college professor in the United States the very next morning.

It was the frightened whinnying of the horses that woke Carver at a little after dawn. It took him some time to come to; at first he couldn't figure out where he was and why his room seemed so cold. Then it all came flooding back to him and he knew that he was camping out. He sat up and looked round groggily, to see what had spooked the horses. To his horror, he found that he was staring straight at the biggest black bear that he had ever seen in his life. It was rearing up on its hind legs, taking what Professor Carver felt to be an unwelcome and disturbing interest in him, his companion and the horses. Carver glanced round and saw that Billy Two Shoes was awake and looking serenely at the bear.

Now, if he'd been sleeping out alone, then Carver would almost certainly have snatched up his rifle and shot at the bear at once. He had in fact shot a bear when he was about fifteen or sixteen, much to his father's delight. The old man had boasted of this achievement to his friends and neighbours, until Joe Carver had grown sick to death of the subject. As a direct consequence, though, of laying there for a couple of hours last night, thinking about the strange powers that an Indian holy man like Billy Two Shoes might possess, Professor Carver did not reach out his hand for the Winchester, but instead looked round at the tree against which the old man had settled himself last night. Incredible as it might seem, Carver was wondering if the Indian had some sort of affinity for the natural world and would be able to speak to the bear in its own language or something of the sort. He said to Billy Two Shoes, 'Are you going to do something about that bear?'

'You're the man with the rifle,' said the Indian and at that same moment the bear, who was not in the best of moods due to having only lately emerged from hibernation, dropped down on to four legs and began to charge towards them. Carver grabbed the rifle lying at his side, cocked it and fired at once. The bullet had no more effect on the three hundred pounds of bone and muscle bearing down on him than if it had been a pea-shooter. He fired again and then once more.

There was no doubt that Carver had hit the beast this time, because a bullet had caused one of the bear's eyes to explode in a welter of blood and jelly. For all the professor knew to the contrary, the bear was already dead, but its momentum still carried it forward. To be on the safe side, he fired twice more and this time, the creature's legs buckled and it faltered. Then it keeled over, rolling towards Carver, who jumped clear just in time. The dead bear came to rest right on the very spot where he had been lying a second or two earlier.

Carver found that his heart was pounding like a steam-hammer and he was breathless with excitement. Surely, nothing of this sort ever happened to him on campus at the college where he taught! Billy Two Shoes got to his feet and walked over to examine the bear. 'You left that late,' was his only observation.

The bear surely was a magnificent specimen. There was not a spare ounce on it; it was nothing but bone, covered in sinew and muscle. 'Those black bears don't often go for people,' said Carver. 'I went out hunting a fair bit with my father and they'd always sooner run than fight.'

'He was hungry,' said Billy Two Shoes. 'Think what

you would do for a meal, if you had not eaten since the fall.'

The Indian went up to the dead animal and felt its fur. Then he pulled open the jaws and examined the teeth. 'When I was a young man,' he said a little wistfully, 'we would have skinned this and taken the head and paws as trophies.'

'I doubt we'll want to burden ourselves with the head, but we could cut some meat off and cook it.'

'You are your father's son. You have a knife?'

Fortunately, Carver had thought to bring an enormous Bowie knife that he had found in his father's workshop. He rolled up his sleeves and after some effort, succeeded in slicing off a number of chunks of lean meat. It wasn't the neatest piece of butchery that he had seen and there seemed to him something slightly degrading about tearing open the bear in that way and leaving it looking bloody and violated. There it was, though.

It didn't take long to kindle a fire and the broiled meat tasted better than any food that Carver could recollect eating over the last ten years. He said, 'I'd forgotten how good fresh food tastes when you're sleeping outside like this.'

'Your father was sad when you went away. He loved to hunt with you at his side.'

'How the deuce do you know that?' asked Carver, a little annoyed to hear his relationship with his father mentioned in this casual way. 'Did he tell you about it?'

'Some he told me, some I guessed,' said Billy Two Shoes imperturbably. 'It was a great sadness to him.'

Rather than explore what was, for Professor Carver, a painful subject, he said, 'How did you know I was coming to see you?'

The old man looked faintly amused. 'Was it so hard to work out?' he asked. 'You come back after all those years and find that you cannot now show your love for your mother and father. What more natural way to make up for it than by chasing after the men who killed them? How many other Indian guides are there near Bluff creek? You needed me.'

Carver thought this over for a bit and then said, 'There's more to the case than that. What's all this about your going on a long journey and going to the tents of your forefathers? You gave me to understand that you'd had some kind of vision of your impending death.'

'Did I?' asked Billy Two Shoes. 'Seems to me I told you I was going to die soon. Visions are nothing to do with it.'

'How do you know, then? That you are going to die soon, I mean.'

The old man did not answer immediately, but then said, 'How often do you listen to your heart?'

'Is that supposed to be metaphysical?' asked Professor Carver, before realizing that the word might not be familiar to an uneducated man. 'What do you mean, "listen to my heart"?'

For the first time since their journey had begun,

Billy Two Shoes laughed. It was not a long belly laugh, more of a brief grunt; but a laugh it had definitely been. 'Your father would not have asked that. You are one of those who wants always to make life hard for your own self. Have you ever listened to your heart?'

Carver decided that the old man was probably more senile than he had known. He answered him patiently, as though speaking to a child, saying, 'No, I don't recall that I ever did.'

'You spend as much time sitting still as I do, you would hear your own heart. Come now, sit here, against a tree.'

The professor allowed himself to be shepherded over to a tree and encouraged to sit up against it. Billy Two Shoes sat down nearby and then they just sat perfectly still for a while. Gradually, as he paid heed to the workings of his own body, Carver became aware of a rumbling in his stomach as the bear meat began to be digested. Then he realized that he could hear the breath entering and leaving his lungs. He had had no occasion to listen to his own breathing for many years. Then, as he settled down and relaxed, he very slowly began to hear a faint singing in his ears. As he attuned to this, he detected a rising and falling; a persistent but almost inaudible susurration, like the waves falling upon an immeasurably distant shore.

The old Indian was watching Professor Carver's face and evidently saw the dawning knowledge that a man could indeed listen to his heart. He said, 'You hear it?'

'I hear my pulse, yes,' said Carver cautiously, 'What of it?'

'I listen all day sometimes to my heart. Four weeks, five weeks ago, I heard a new sound. My heart is failing. Every day it gets weaker and there are strange noises deep within. Soon, my heart will stop.'

'Is that it?' asked Professor Carver, feeling vaguely cheated. 'You didn't receive a message from the spirit world?'

'No. Just listened to my heart is all.'

After spending a wretched day in the cave and then sleeping there, all on exceedingly short commons, Patrick Tarleton wasn't sorry when Morgan and Sutter somehow agreed to try somewhere else to stay. They talked the matter over; largely leaving Tarleton out of their conversation.

'You know "Crusher" Frobisher's place?' asked Sutter. 'Little cantina and trading post?'

'I been there,' said Morgan. 'Didn't think a whole lot of it, tell you the truth. Why d'you ask?'

'I know Frobisher a little, from long time back. I reckon as he might be inclined to let us sleep in his hay-loft, if we spend a little at his establishment.'

'Hay-loft, eh? Sounds like it couldn't be worse than this cave. How far from here?'

Sutter thought for a moment and said, 'Half a day's ride.'

'You think he'll have vittles there?'

'It's his stock in trade. He lives with a squaw, almost gone Indian himself. But there'll be food and drink, make no doubt about that.'

As they gathered their gear together, Sutter said casually to Tarleton, 'You comin'?'

'Sure. Thought we'd to stick together anyway. Safety in numbers and suchlike.' In fact, Patrick Tarleton was more than half minded to strike out by himself. He just didn't know how the others would take it. He had seen two of their party shot dead in the course of a few days and although he supposed that he couldn't lay the blame for Flynn's death at their door, it did seem that riding with Sutter and Morgan was what one might term a high-risk occupation.

It was a pleasant enough ride to Frobisher's place. Tarleton had been in the territories before, but only to pass through. This was the first time that he had holed up there for a while, though, and he wasn't taking to the experience in any way at all. Perhaps it might have been different if he was in the company of men who he liked and trusted, but that was very far from being the case with Jed Sutter and Jack Morgan.

Scattered across the Indian Nations were various enterprises run by white men who thought that they might be able to make their fortunes from exploiting the Redskins. It was a rare man who managed to do more than scrape a bare living out of such businesses.

Some sold tinware and other goods to the Indians; bartering them in exchange for pelts. Others traded in liquor, which was technically illegal in the territories. There was also a lively trade in firearms. Most, like 'Crusher' Frobisher, managed after years of endeavour to do little more than grub out a living, hand to mouth, by combining all these activities.

Pete Frobisher lived in a stone-built, two-storey dwelling house, against the wall of which was a wooden lean-to which served as a place where passing white men could obtain food and a drink. Near the house were a few other buildings, these being constructed of wood; a barn, outhouse, sheds and so on. Every January 1st, Frobisher promised himself that this would be the year that he made his fortune. Sometimes, he dreamed of uncovering the location of some lost and fabulously rich gold mine. At other times, he imagined that some passing traveller might drop dead nearby and prove to be in the possession of half a million dollars in cash money. In the meantime, he scraped by from day to day, making just about enough to keep him and his Indian wife from going too hungry.

Sutter and Morgan had led the way to Frobisher's trading post, Patrick Tarleton not having the remotest idea where he was or really knowing anything at all about the territories, other than that he wished devoutly to be out of them and back in civilized lands again. Two things prevented him from striking out alone. First off was that he did not fancy roaming alone through the Indian Nations. He had a tidy sum of money now in his saddle-bag and he was a man who had in the past seen murder committed for a tenth of the amount that he was currently carrying. Then again, he was by no means sure that Sutter and Morgan would actually agree to his parting company from them. He had no desire to end up like Emile Beauregarde.

The second reason why Tarleton thought it expedient to stick with the other two men, at least for the time being, was this: it was still a little under a week since they had killed the sheriff in Bluff Creek. Sometimes, these small towns were that keen on their local dignitaries that they would go to almost superhuman lengths to avenge them. If, by some chance, there was still a posse on their tail, then he would sooner encounter it in the company of ruthless killers like Sutter and Morgan than be taken alone.

The bar or eating house or whatever you cared to call it at Frobisher's was tiny and cramped. There was room, at most, for perhaps a dozen or so souls to sit eating and drinking. Although if that many men had been there, they would have needed to keep their elbows down and not move about too much, for fear of jogging their neighbours. There were four mean little tables and ten chairs. In addition to the chairs, there were three sections of sawn log, which performed the function of stools when the place was crowded. At one end of the poky little room were two barrels, with planks laid across them. Behind these planks there usually stood either 'Crusher' Frobisher or his squaw, serving food and drink.

There were four men clustered around one table when Sutter and the others arrived. These four men gave one the impression of being close friends or associates. They sat huddled together and leaning forward so that their conversation was soft and secret. Morgan cast his eyes casually over this group and realized that he knew one of them. The man didn't know him, though, for which Jed Sutter was thankful.

Three months back, Sutter had been passing the sheriff's office in a Texas town called Purchase. There was a crooked deputy there who sometimes gave him tips about likely jobs in exchange for a cut of the proceeds, naturally. He had seen a man leaving the office; a man with a very distinctive scar all down the side of his face. It looked like he had been badly burned or something. When he later met up with the deputy, Sutter asked out of curiosity about the fellow he had seen.

'There's a man you don't want to get crosswise to,' the deputy had replied, with great feeling. 'Name of Clayton, Ebeneezer Clayton. A meaner son of a bitch never walked the earth.'

'Who is he? What does he do?' Sutter had asked.

'Do? He's a bounty killer. Hunts men down and brings back their corpses for the cash reward. Some men, they bring men back alive sometimes, other times dead. Clayton never yet brought back a living man. Most times, the bodies he brings in have bullets in the back and suchlike. We reckon as he just hunts 'em down and shoots 'em from ambush.'

And now this self-same man was sitting right there at a table with three other fellows, who looked to Sutter as though they were very likely in a similar line of work to Clayton. It was a tricky dilemma that they now faced. To have bolted from Frobisher's as soon as they walked through the door would have looked mighty suspicious to those men sitting there. They most likely weren't looking for the men who had killed the sheriff of Bluff Creek, but there was every chance that their curiosity would be aroused by a display of fear and the appearance of flight. The best thing to do was probably to brazen it out and hope that Clayton and his boys lit out soon.

CHAPTER 7

The trouble with being an outlaw is that you never really know who might or might not wish you dead or be minded to lay hands on you in order to claim any reward available for bringing you to justice. While Sutter, Morgan and Tarleton were fretting about the regular law and perhaps giving half a mind to bounty hunters, they hadn't for a moment thought that the son of the man they had shot down would be on their trail. That two other men would have sworn a solemn oath to see them dead, would not have crossed their minds for a moment.

The young man that Beauregarde had so needlessly shot was called Dull Knife and he was seventeen years of age. The other two Cherokees who had been with him at the time were about the same age and their names were Little Feather and Horse-Born. Horse-Born was Dull Knife's younger brother by a year or so. They had no particular purpose in drifting up to that hut where the four white men were hiding out; it was just high spirits and mischief. They certainly hadn't meant any harm to the men. Young men will always find ways of getting into scrapes, though, whatever their colour or creed; although nobody could have foreseen that in this case, death would be the result.

The bullet that had hit Dull Knife's upper thigh did not seem to have caused any great mischief. Blood was oozing from the wound, rather than flowing freely and with the aid of his brother and friend, Dull Knife was able to make it back to the settlement without too much trouble. It looked to them all as though this was no more than a clean flesh wound and that once the bullet was removed, it should heal up with no difficulty. What none of them knew was that the ball had nicked the main artery in the young man's right leg and was now effectively plugging the wound and preventing blood loss.

When they got back to their homes, Little Feather went off to fetch the Healer; an old woman who acted as the clan's doctor. She inserted a probe into Dull Knife's wound, hooked out the bullet and then watched in dismay as a fountain of blood erupted. The young man's blood pressure dropped rapidly, he complained of being cold, lapsed into unconsciousness and died within the hour from massive blood loss.

The unexpected death of a youth was by no means an uncommon occurrence in the Cherokee village. Most such deaths, though, were as a consequence of hunting accidents or perhaps skirmishes with members of other tribes; there being historic enmity between the Cherokee and Choctaw. This was different. These white men had no business to be in their district anyway. While they were living peaceably nearby for a few days and trading with the clan, they had been tolerated. Now, things had changed.

There was no question of an attempt to exact vengeance on the man who had killed their friend until the funeral ceremonies for Dull Knife had been completed. Because he had died in the village, there was no reason at all to delay these proceedings and so the wailing and keening of his female relatives began that very afternoon and continued long into the night. Little Feather and Horse-Born took part, according to custom, but their minds were less occupied with religious observance than with how quickly they would be able to slip away and attack the men who had deprived them of their comrade.

Guns were expensive, too expensive for two youths of their age to be able to afford, and so Little Feather and Horse-Born slipped out in the middle of the night, armed with bows, knives and lances. They took with them their ponies and enough provisions for three days. They did not believe that it would take them that long to track down and kill the white men. Young as they were, they had already taken part in more than one battle and both had killed men before. True, the men they were hunting had guns, but they did not know the lay of the land the way that these young warriors did. The Indians had another powerful reason to succeed in their quest; a motive wholly lacking in the white men. This was an affair of honour. If they did not either avenge Dull Knife's death or die in the attempt, they would be shamed forever. He had been their battle-comrade and blood-brother and it was their sacred duty now to make sure that blood answered for blood.

Professor Carver and Billy Two Shoes arrived at the Cherokee village in the aftermath of Dull Knife's death. By the time they got there, it was known that Little Feather and Horse-Born had gone after the killers to call them to account. There had not been a blood feud against white men for some time and so the vendetta had a certain novelty value. It was the topic of general conversation in the Indian settlement, until people saw two riders approaching. One of them was a white man, which might have boded ill for the man, if somebody had not recognized the old man on the pony next to him.

To Carver's astonishment, the entire village gradually fell silent, as people stopped what they were doing and turned to face him and Billy Two Shoes. The old man didn't seem at all thrown by this, merely remarking in a casual aside, 'It is many years since I came here.'

The Cherokee settlement was not at all like any sort of village with which the professor was acquainted. For one thing, the only structures were wigwams of branches and skins; very similar to the one in which his guide had lately been living. Another difference was that these dwelling places were not arranged in straight lines, as one would expect in a white town; but were instead scattered about, apparently at random. The overall impression was, to Carver's eye at least, haphazard and higgledy-piggledy. There did not appear to be any order in the place.

At first, Professor Carver expected to be left out of the greetings and to have little idea what was going on, but he had reckoned without Billy Two Shoes' innate courtesy and his sense of what was fitting. The old man said something in Cherokee and then turned to Carver, saying, 'I have told them that you are my friend and that it is polite to speak English in front of you.'

Carver felt monumentally embarrassed by this, but at the same time sensible that he was being paid a great honour.

'Welcome back, Chief,' said a handsome man of perhaps forty. 'It is many years since we saw you.'

'I am happy to see my people once more,' said Billy Two Shoes. 'It is only for a little time. I will soon die.'

This bluntness was so alien to anything that the professor could conceive of in his normal life, that he almost choked on hearing this plain statement of fact. The former Chief continued, 'I told this white man that I would help him find the men who killed his father. I cannot do this now, because death is waiting at my side. Now I ask that somebody will help this young man on the trail. He seeks four white men.'

There was some shuffling at this, accompanied by exchanges of sidelong glances. If I didn't know better, thought Carver, I should say that these people know more about this than I do. He decided that it would be much better if Billy Two Shoes were able to speak to his people in their own language and so Carver said quietly, 'Listen, sir, I am obliged to you for all this, but you and your friends must have a lot of catching up to do. If you don't mind, I'll take a turn round this place and get to know folk a little.'

The old man smiled at Carver and said, 'We will meet soon.' Trying to slip out of the scene with as little fuss and bother as possible, Carver dismounted and led his horse away, so that Billy Two Shoes and his people could say what they needed to each other.

All the adults, maybe fifty or sixty of them, had gathered around his travelling companion and the only ones who showed no interest in the return of a man who had been absent for twenty or thirty years, were the children. For them, the presence of a white man in the village was a far greater and more entertaining novelty. They clustered round Carver, chattering and laughing.

'I'm sorry,' he said, 'but I can't understand a single word of what you little ones are saying.' The children did not appear to be at all bothered by the fact that neither party in the conversation could make head nor tail of what the other was saying and they continued to talk in an animated way. For his own part, Professor Carver said such things as, 'Delighted to meet you, I'm sure!' and, 'It's very kind of you to say so,' and various other remarks which would have been more suited to a soirée held by his city friends.

Frobisher greeted Sutter like an old friend. 'Jed, you bastard, what're you doing in these parts? Ain't seen you in the longest time.'

'Ah, you know how it is. Just passing through. Any chance of some food?'

'Sure. What'll it be? Pork and beans or beans and pork?'

This was an old joke of Crusher's and Sutter gave a brief smile. 'You don't change much over the years, Frobisher,' he observed. 'How's that wife o' yours?'

'Fair to middlin', fair to middlin'. Really, what are you doing round here? Up to mischief?'

With a notorious bounty killer sitting a matter of feet away, this was precisely the sort of conversation which Jed Sutter had been hoping to avoid. He contented himself with saying, 'Frobisher, you always think the worst o' folk. We ain't up to any mischief. Just passing through.'

'If you say so,' said 'Crusher' Frobisher, dubiously. 'I guess there's a first time for everything.'

The four men at the other table were a softly spoken crew; talking quietly in voices so low that not

97

a word could be heard by Sutter, Morgan and Tarleton. If it hadn't been for this, Sutter would have warned the two men with him that they should not say anything which might attract unfavourable attention. As it was, the only conversation from Morgan and Tarleton concerned their appetites and how delighted they would be to have a good, cooked meal.

It was while they were tucking into their food that things took a turn for the worse. Trading posts such as Frobisher's were often good spots for men on the scout to pick up with others of similar inclinations, so that they could band together for jobs which needed a bit of strength. Obviously, one needed to be a little cautious about this and it was not until strangers had had a chance to gauge each other, that direct discussion of criminal enterprises might take place. Sutter was therefore not a little alarmed when one of the men at the other table said, 'Hey, you boys there! You want a little action?'

Knowing, as he did, that one of these characters was a bounty hunter made it all but a racing certainty that this gambit was intended to sound out Sutter, Morgan and Tarleton and see if they were up to no good. The others looked at Sutter questioningly, as much as to say, 'How do we play this?' He turned to the other table and said in a polite but somewhat puzzled tone, 'I'm not sure I understand you. What kind of action you talkin' about?'

The man who had spoken was, Sutter saw with a

sinking heart, the one he knew to be a bounty hunter. He and his three companions looked as though they were all cut from the same piece of cloth; tough, capable men of the kind who would draw down on you at the drop of a hat. The bounty hunter said, 'Just wondered if you fellows wanted to play a few hands of cards. Why, what did you think I meant?'

'No idea. We'll pass on the cards, though, but thanks anyway.'

'Where you heading?'

'I reckon that's our business,' said Sutter. 'Don't want to be unfriendly, but me and my partners keep ourselves to ourselves.'

'So you ain't the friendly sort?'

'Not so's you'd notice, no,' said Sutter. He didn't want to go up against those men right now, especially since they were four to his three and although he knew Morgan was quick enough with a pistol, he had his doubts about young Tarleton. Still and all, it was against Jed Sutter's nature to allow anybody to push him around and if this man was set upon going up against him, well then he guessed he'd just have to accommodate him.

Matters seemed to pass off smoothly, though, with the bounty hunter saying regretfully, 'That's a real shame. Nothing like a game of cards to bring men together.' Then he stood up and stretched. The other three men at the table also got to their feet and they all trooped outside. At first, Sutter breathed a sigh of relief, believing that the whole episode had ended and that they could now relax. That was until he saw the four men strolling casually over to the horses belonging to him, Morgan and Tarleton.

The planks which formed the walls of the little room in which they were sitting were not slotted tightly together, making it damned drafty in there when the wind was blowing outside. This also meant that from inside, you could see a lot of what was passing on the other side of the wall. Added to this, none of the four men who had just left had bothered closing the door. It looked to Sutter like they didn't even care if he and his companions saw what they were about.

It was the contempt shown for them by the casual way that the four men had gone straight over and started inspecting his horse, that provoked Sutter to murderous rage. In itself, he might still have held back from action; after all, he had not lived as long as he had by reacting madly and irrationally to every slight and provocation. It was when he glimpsed one of the men peering into the saddle-bags that Sutter knew things had gone past the point of no return. And even as this realization struck him, his mind was running fast to figure out the best way of maximizing their edge against the four men outside. He had no illusions at all about the kind of men they were. If it came to a straight gunfight between those four and Sutter and his two partners, then they were altogether lost.

'On your feet, you two,' said Sutter urgently. 'Quickly now.'

'What's to do?' asked Morgan, a little suspiciously. He might be working a double act with Sutter, but that wasn't to say that he particularly trusted the fellow.

'Come on,' said Sutter, 'those men are bounty hunters and they've just been looking at our baggage. Draw your pieces.'

As they moved towards the open door, as though to confront the men outside, Sutter positioned himself fractionally behind Tarleton. The men had left off examining their horses and saddle-bags now and were heading back towards the bar. One way or another, there was going to be blood shed in the next few seconds. When they had almost reached the door, Sutter gave Tarleton an almighty great shove, which sent the young man stumbling out into the bright light of day. He stood for an instant, dazzled and a little bewildered by the push that he had received. Inside the lean-to, Sutter said to Morgan, 'Fire through the cracks. It's us or them.' The other man understood the play at once and hurried to the wooden wall.

Meanwhile, 'Crusher' Frobisher had also twigged what was afoot and was crying out, 'No, no Sutter. Stop now, for Christ's sake. . . .' His frantic pleading was cut off sharply by the roar of gunfire, from both inside and outside the wooden structure.

Throwing Patrick Tarleton out like that had been

101

a right smart move, because when Sutter and Morgan began firing, the only target that the four men outside could immediately identify was the young man with a gun in his hand. All of them started shooting at Tarleton. Sutter and Morgan were invisible, of course, being hidden behind the wall of the lean-to. The men at whom they were firing could not at once see where the shooting was coming from and by the time they stopped shooting at Tarleton and tried to work out just whereabouts in the bar Sutter and Morgan might be, it was too late. The two of them were able to kill the bounty hunter and every one of his friends.

When the shooting was over, Sutter cried loudly, 'Hooey! It was like a turkey shoot. Every one of those whore's sons down.'

Morgan was still not quite sure what had happened, other than the fact that he had succeeded in killing two men, without suffering a scratch himself. Frobisher was pretty wild about the whole thing and made no effort to hide his displeasure. 'Sutter,' he shouted, purple with fury, 'what the hell have you done? Are you plumb crazy?'

They all three of them went outside to look at the aftermath of the massacre. The first body was that of Patrick Tarleton. He lay so close to the door that they had to step over him. Tarleton was riddled with bullet holes; it was clear that almost every shot that the four men had fired had been at the young man. It was hardly surprising, really, since he was the only target that they could actually see. Morgan spoke the eulogy, saying, 'He wasn't a bad kid.'

'Well, he's no use to us or himself now,' said Sutter.

One of the horses was lying on its side, whinnying pitifully. It had caught a stray bullet in one of its legs. Sutter went over and put the creature out of its misery, the sound of the shot echoing back from the nearby hills.

The four men who had been sitting at the table when Sutter and Morgan arrived were all dead. It had been, as Sutter earlier remarked, a turkey shoot. Those men hadn't even known where the bullets were coming from. They'd been so busy firing at the young man with a gun in his hand, they hadn't even had time to figure out that two men hiding in the gloomy bar were the ones that they should be concerning themselves with.

'We'll have to rid ourselves of these bodies,' said Frobisher, in a matter-of-fact way. 'Somebody finds them here and I'm apt to get my neck stretched.'

'Get rid o' them?' asked Morgan. 'Where d'you say we should put them?'

'The river,' said Frobisher, so promptly that the other two men suspected that this means had been used in the past to dispose of inconvenient corpses.

The river ran about a quarter mile from Frobisher's house. The three of them used the dead men's horses and loaded them up with the mortal remains of their former owners. Then they led them along to the river.

Luckily for their purpose, the recent storms had turned the sometimes sluggish water-course into a foaming torrent. The flow would be sure to carry the incriminating evidence far from Frobisher's door. One by one, they dropped the bodies in and watched them being carried away by the rushing waters. All of them had blood on their hands by the time they had undertaken this unpleasant task and so they rinsed their hands in the icy water.

'What about they horses?' asked Morgan. 'Turn 'em loose or shoot them as well?'

'Let's get anything from 'em as'd tell folks who they belonged to,' said Frobisher, who was hoping to turn a profit on this business. He had been mightily vexed at Sutter for starting the shooting, but was now determined to make the best of a bad job. If there was any money or anything else of value in the saddle-bags, he figured he was entitled to a half share.

The only items of interest in the first of the saddle-bags they rifled was a sheaf of wanted bills. These were covered in spidery and cryptic notes, which they took to be information about current whereabouts of the subjects of the posters. On one, for example, was scribbled, 'Left Topeka, end of March. Some say heading south'. On another, was written, 'Dead'.

'Bounty hunters, maybe?' said Frobisher, 'I hates 'em like the plague. Bastards.'

'They was bounty hunters all right,' said Sutter and filled in the others about what he knew of at least one of the party.

The other saddle-bags yielded nearly two hundred dollars in gold, which, it was agreed, 'Crusher' Frobisher should take as recompense for the trouble they had caused him. The horses were turned loose, still tacked up, to wander where they would. There was nothing hereabouts now to bring the crime home to this area. Those men could have been killed anywhere in the territories.

CHAPTER 8

There was a feast that night in the Cherokee village, to celebrate the return of their one-time Chief. Professor Carver never really worked out what had happened and why the man whom he knew as Billy Two Shoes should have abandoned his own people and taken up residence north of Bluff Creek. Was it a penance, a call from God, expiation of some ancient crime? He never found out.

He never knew either what the old Chief had told the people in the village concerning him. All that Carver knew was that he was treated with great courtesy and assigned a wikiup to himself. He supposed that he would learn in due season how things would pan out.

The children whose acquaintance Carver had made, stuck to him. They didn't see all that many white people and they wanted to make the most of it. It didn't seem to bother them at all that they could not make any sense of what the professor was saying to them and he in turn found them agreeable company, despite the language difficulties.

Towards nightfall, a messenger came for Carver. This was a tall young fellow of about twenty years of age. He spoke passable English and said, 'I have come to take you to your friend.'

Old Billy Two Shoes was sitting cross-legged on the ground in front of a small fire. It was not, by the look of it, a cooking fire and Carver supposed that this one had been lit just to keep the old man warm. Around the old Indian was a crowd of maybe twenty men, all sitting patiently, as though Billy Two Shoes had been teaching school or something. He greeted the professor in his usual, calm manner and then said, 'I find that I cannot go with you to help you find those men.'

Carver began to mumble some conventional expression of regret, something along the lines of, 'Oh, I'm sorry to hear that, sir . . .' But the old man continued: 'There is not much time. My heart will stop tonight or tomorrow. I will stay here to die.'

Carver was genuinely sorry to hear this and tried to find the words to convey this to Billy Two Shoes. The old man raised his hand and said, 'Yes, I too am sorry. This boy,' he indicated the young messenger, 'this boy is my daughter's son's son. He will help you.'

'Thank you, sir . . ' said Carver.

'Go now,' said the Chief, 'I have words to speak to my people. I wish you good fortune.'

It was a dismissal as gracious as that which might be spoken by a prince or cardinal and Carver withdrew quietly, accompanied by the man who he understood to be Billy Two Shoes' great grandson. As they walked back to the wikiup where Carver assumed that he would be sleeping that night, he said to the man at his side, 'My name is Joseph Carver. How do they call you?'

'I am known as Runner. When I was a child, I ran everywhere.'

'And you will help me track the men I am looking for, is that right?'

'They may be dead now.'

'Hey, how's that? Have you seen them?'

Runner stopped walking and said, 'Others had a blood feud with some men. Perhaps those you seek.'

'I'm sorry,' said Professor Carver, 'but you've lost me now. What are you talking about?'

Briefly, Runner told the story of the four men who had been living nearby and how one of them had killed Dull Knife. 'Now Dull Knife's brother and his friend have gone off to see if they can kill the men. I think that these are the same men that you want to find.'

The professor rubbed his chin thoughtfully. 'Well, I suppose that you will still help me to track these white men down?'

'Yes, of course. I made a promise. We can start tomorrow morning.'

*

Little Feather and Horse-Born were genuinely grieved about the loss of a brother and friend, but at the same time, the two young men were aware that they were embarking upon an heroic quest of the kind beloved of their people. If they could avenge Dull Knife's death, then they would win respect not only in their own clan, but throughout the whole Cherokee Nation. This was the stuff of songs around the fire at night; how two youngsters, barely more than boys, hunted down and killed the armed men who had snuffed out the life of their comrade.

They might have been angry and excitable young fellows, but neither Little Feather nor Horse-Born were fools. They knew well enough that it would be madness for them to confront the killers and engage to fight them upon their own terms. Some of the white men, they knew, followed a strange set of customs which they called the 'Rattlesnake Code'. This forbade a man from shooting an enemy in the back or even attacking without first sending a signal of defiance. The young Indians found such a system utterly incomprehensible. Warfare and murder were not games that you played according to some foolish book of rules. There was only one rule: kill your enemy or die at his hands.

As they made their way to the hut where the white men had been staying, the two men agreed that they would do their best to pick off the men with their bows, firing without warning. They were both skilled and accomplished hunters, able to creep up and surprise even the most timid of prey. If they could close in on and kill a gazelle, before it was even aware of their presence, then it should not be too hard to get within striking range of some stupid, clumsy white men. It was well known that the white man had no more awareness of his surroundings than a rock or tree.

It came as no surprise to either of the men that the hut was deserted now. The mud around the ramshackle building, though, told a clear and accurate tale of hasty departure. The tracks of four horses, clearly shod by white men, were as clear as could be and they pointed west. Little Feather and Horse-Born remounted their ponies and set off in pursuit.

Later that day, the trail led to a cave in the side of a section of river-cliff. The two Cherokees soon found Beauregarde's corpse, lying where he had fallen. To their delight, they found that the body had not been looted. There was a pistol in the dead man's hand and another in a holster at his hip. Both were fully loaded. This was booty indeed!

Little Feather and Horse-Born discussed the new situation briefly. They recognized Beauregarde at once as the man who had shot and killed Dull Knife. Since he was dead, did that mean that they should now end their journey and return home? Neither of them had any appetite for this course of action. There would be something faintly humiliating and ridiculous, after setting out so proudly, to return without shedding any blood. Besides, the white men

110

had all been to blame for this man's actions. Not only that, but the odds had now shortened in favour of the Indians. There were now three men to kill, rather than four. And, best of all, the hunters had firearms of their own, in addition to their bows and lances. They set off west again, more determined than ever to find and kill the remaining white men.

All things considered, thought Sutter, Frobisher had taken the shootout fairly well. True, he had been very angry at first, but once he had calmed down, it was clear that the two hundred dollars in gold which he had reaped from the affair had gone a long way to placating him. He wasn't best pleased about having his establishment turned into a battlefield, but had decided that there was no real harm done. Frobisher loathed bounty hunters as much as the next man and the news that the dead men had belonged to that despicable breed had also caused him to take a more relaxed view of the massacre.

'Don't you ever pull a stunt like this here again, Sutter,' he grumbled. 'I damn near put my back out, hoisting those bastards up on to they horses. Jesus!'

'There was bound to be blood spilled, one way or another,' said Sutter reasonably. 'You'd o' sooner that any old friend like me came out alive, I'll bet.'

'Just don't do it again. My nerves wouldn't stand it. I thought I would o' died of shock when you and your partner here started shooting.'

'Sometimes these things just happen,' said

Morgan. 'No point fussin' 'bout it.'

Frobisher looked pardonably annoyed at this casual dismissal of a gun battle which had resulted in no fewer than five fatalities. 'Is that what you call this?' he asked wrathfully, 'just me fussin'?'

'Don't take on,' said Sutter. 'He didn't mean nothing by it.'

They were sitting outside Frobisher's house. He had insisted on their bringing out some chairs from the bar, claiming that the stink of the gunpowder aggravated his asthma. 'I suppose you boys are wanting to sleep here or something, am I right?' asked Crusher shrewdly. 'I knew you two were on the run. I ain't stupid, you know.'

'Never thought you were,' said Sutter.

'You fellows tell me what you're really about now and I might be able to help,' said Frobisher. 'Not that I'm promising, mind.'

'We want to keep down here in the territories for a week or two. Nothing more to it than that,' Morgan said. 'Thought we might stay in your barn for a few nights.'

Frobisher considered this proposition, his greedy mind working out what advantage he might be able to make of it. At length, he said, 'I can do better than that old barn. You two make it worth my while, you can sleep right in the house. Got a spare room there. Only one bed, but it's a big'un. You could both fit in. You can have cooked meals and everything else. Hell, I don't mind, you want to eat with me and my squaw.'

Sutter and Morgan looked at each other, both a little surprised by this proposal. It was certainly an attractive idea, sleeping in a bed and being indoors again. The thought of regular cooked meals, eaten at a table, was also an alluring one. Sutter said, 'You'll want us to pay handsomely for all this, I reckon?'

'I ain't a priest or aught, Sutter. Of course I'll want payin'. What the hell d'you think? I rent you a room and get my wife to do your cooking, I'll want paying well. It'd be the same if'n you went to any town, I suppose.'

What Frobisher didn't say was that trade was exceedingly slack just then and that the men that had been slaughtered just a few hours earlier had been his first customers in better than a week. Even the Cherokee seemed for some reason to be keeping away and it was all he could do to make ends meet. The gold he'd taken from the bounty hunters' bags was useful, but having a couple of paying guests for a fortnight would surely help tide him over until things picked up a little, which they generally did in the spring.

'All right,' said Sutter suddenly, 'me and my partner here'll take you up on your offer and thanking you kindly for it.'

Not wanting to give the men a chance of repenting of their acceptance, Frobisher said, 'Bring your bags into the house now and I'll tend to your horses after.'

Little Feather and Horse-Born followed the tracks of

the white men's horses west. They kept going even after the sun had set and the moon risen. There was only this one track and white men were notorious for keeping to roads and tracks. It led them, by perhaps ten that night, to a stone building, surrounded by barns and a corral. There were lights on in the house and the sound of men's voices, shouting and laughing drunkenly.

The two Indians slipped into the corral and examined the hoofs of the horses there, satisfying themselves that these were the ones that they had been following. It was a fair guess that the owners were now in the nearby house. The young men retreated to a rise of ground, crowned with a ring of stunted silver birches, which gave an uninterrupted view down to the house. Then they lay down to sleep, confident that they would be able to kill the men they had tracked, as soon as they emerged from the house.

It had been a heavy night. Not only was Frobisher happy to provide cooked food for Sutter and Morgan, he was free with his liquor as well. True, they would be paying for all this, but then they surely weren't short of money at the moment. Crusher could be an agreeable host when the mood was upon him and he wasn't sorry to have new faces about the house. Times were never too prosperous in the winter and he and his wife grew pretty sick of each other's company by the spring. This wasn't the first time that Frobisher had, on an impulse, invited men to stay at his house in this way.

The three men had drunk themselves stupid that night and all of them woke the next day with headaches and raging thirsts. Frobisher's squaw was up and about the kitchen at the same early hour as usual, but the men slumbered through until an hour before noon. Sutter woke first and then felt so dreadful that he didn't see why Morgan shouldn't wake up too and share his misery. They were both sprawled in the same double bed and so Sutter simply kicked his partner's leg, saying, 'Wake up there, you lazy cow's son.'

Morgan opened his eyes and said, 'Jesus, I feel terrible.'

'It's that stuff as Frobisher was fetching from the barn. I mind he has a still there. Moonshine often has this effect on me.'

'You think his wife would have cooked our breakfast by now?'

'Well,' said Sutter, 'if she has, I doubt she'll be bringing it to us in bed. We'd best go down to the kitchen and see how things are shaping up.'

Sutter and Morgan threw on their clothes and stumbled, bleary-eyed, down the passage to the stairs. A door opened as they passed and Frobisher peered out, saying, 'What are you bastards up to?'

'Lookin' for breakfast.'

'It's awful early. Wait, though, I'll come down with you. Don't want you alarming my woman.'

Morgan said, 'What was that rotgut you was feeding us with last night? Was it moonshine?'

Frobisher winked. 'Ah, you may say so, boys. When there's no passing business from villains like you men, there's always demand from the Redskins for firewater.'

There was no sign of Frobisher's wife in the kitchen, which irritated him. He said, 'I'd o' thought she'd have vittles goin' for us by now. Maybe she's out back somewhere. I'll go look.'

'We'll come with you,' said Sutter. 'I could do with some fresh air, you know. Sorry to have to tell you, Frobisher, but this house o' yourn ain't exactly the sweetest-smelling abode I ever been in!'

'You find yourself a nice, clean hotel, then,' said Frobisher, irritably. 'You was glad enough of my offer to stay yesterday.'

The three men ambled out of the kitchen door and into the yard behind the house. It was a glorious spring morning; the whole scene before them was bathed in golden sunshine. 'Surely is good to be alive on a day such as this!' said Frobisher, stretching his arms above his head and yawning. These were, by a great irony, the very last words that 'Crusher' Frobisher spoke in his life. An arrow came sailing through the air and went straight through his throat; the razor-sharp flint head emerging from the back of his neck.

For a moment, Frobisher stood there, with that arrow in his neck, looking faintly surprised at the turn of events. Then he began coughing and choking; a great crimson gout of blood spilling from his mouth and over his shirt front. Both Sutter and Morgan might have been suffering the after-effects of a prolonged drinking session of poor-quality poteen, but their reactions were not dulled. Both of them hurled themselves to the ground, just as two more arrows thudded into the kitchen door and its wooden frame. Wasting no more time, the men dived back into the house and without saying a word to each other, ran up the stairs to fetch their guns.

Professor Carver enjoyed the feast, although he kept himself very much in the background and hardly spoke to anybody. He was very conscious that this was Billy Two Shoes' special celebration; something like a retirlement party, crossed with a wake was the best way that Carver could characterize the event. Some of the children sat with Carver and chattered; every so often, he would make a remark in English, which caused them to fall about laughing.

By what Carver judged to be about midnight, though, he had had enough of the experience. It can be wearisome to listen too long to speeches and songs in a language which you do not understand and he was in any case dog-tired. He slipped away from the assembly and found his way to the wikiup which had been assigned to him. Within a few minutes of laying his head down, Carver was fast asleep.

The man who had introduced himself as 'Runner', came to wake the professor up at dawn. It was a chilly time and Carver could happily have spent another few hours dozing. Nevertheless, he thought that it would be rude to keep Runner waiting and so he got up and gathered his bits and pieces together. He said to Runner, 'That was some feast that you held last night. Your Chief must be pleased that you all made such a thing of his coming back here.'

'Yes, he was very happy. It was a good time to die.'

At first, Professor Carver thought that he must have misheard the young Indian or perhaps the man had used the wrong English word by mistake. Carver said, 'I'm sorry, I didn't catch that?'

'I said,' Runner repeated in the same even and unemotional tone of voice, 'it was a good time to die.'

'He's dead? When did this happen?'

'During the feast. He said that his heart would fail and it failed. We did not notice at first, because the Chief was sitting up. He did not fall over when his heart stopped its beating. Just carried on sitting there, with his eyes open.'

'I'm so sorry,' said Carver. 'I suppose you won't want to be leaving here for a bit now.'

'We will leave as soon as we have eaten. It was what my ancestor wished.'

Curious, thought Carver, that as soon as Billy Two Shoes was dead, he became an 'ancestor', rather than the great grandfather he had been before. Out

loud, he said, 'Won't there be mourning and suchlike?'

'He did not want it. My ancestor said that we
should leave the dead to care for the dead.'

Professor Carver and Runner left the village half
an hour later, after breaking their fast upon some
unleavened bread, washed down with draughts of
spring water. Runner assured him that the pony that
Billy Two Shoes had ridden could safely be left at the
settlement.

Runner was an agreeable enough companion,
although no more talkative than any other Indian.
Carver asked him where he had learned such good
English.

'The missioners taught me. My mother sent me to
stay at a Christian school when I was younger. She
said that no man could live a good life in this country
now without being able to speak English.'

'There might be truth somewhat in that,' said
Carver. 'It's a pity, but I think that your mother was
perfectly correct.'

'What are we to do,' asked Runner, 'when we find
the men who killed your father? If my friends have
not already killed them.'

'I'll level with you, Runner,' said Carver, 'and tell
you that I don't rightly know what I will do. I don't
know if I am able to shoot men in cold blood, always
assuming that they consent to stand around quietly
and let me do so. I suppose the civilized thing would
be to take them into custody and return them to

Bluff Creek, where the murder was done, you know, to face justice. But the truth is, I just don't know.'

So bound up in the pursuit had Carver been, that this was the first time in over twenty-four hours that he had been asked to consider what the ultimate purpose of this little jaunt might be. It had begun as a way of mitigating his guilt for the way that he had neglected his parents over the last years and had certainly proved most eminently successful in that regard. The burden of guilt had slipped away and he had scarcely even thought of his mother and father since leaving Bluff Creek. Still, he supposed that the matter would eventually reach some kind of resolution, but what that would be; he had not the faintest idea.

From the speed with which those arrows had arrived, especially the second and third, which had struck the woodwork almost simultaneously, Sutter and Morgan both concluded that there must be at least two or three Indians outside the house. It was not hard to deduce that they were after blood. Both men had thought that this might have some connection with the young Indian that Beauregarde had shot, but it might equally well be some men that Frobisher had pissed off in the past. Against that theory was the fact that even when Frobisher had caught an arrow through his throat, the attack had continued. On balance, it was probably Sutter and Morgan themselves who were the targets of vengeance.

Having made such a good start and evened the odds in the forthcoming fight to two against two; Little Feather and Horse-Born now made a deadly tactical mistake. With their bows, they were accurate and could, as evidenced by the death of 'Crusher' Frobisher, kill at a considerable distance. Neither man, though, was very familiar with firearms. Both of them had fired rifles and scatterguns in the past, but pistols were something of a novelty for them. The thrill of owning such exciting weapons was too much of a temptation for them and they chose to continue the assault on the house with Beauregarde's twin Remingtons, rather than the more reliable long distance weapons with which they were familiar and proficient.

Both the white men in the house had buckled on their gunbelts and picked up the rifles that they had left leaning against the wall in a corner of the room. The Winchesters were sighted up to a thousand yards, but the men who had fired those arrows were nothing like as far away. Standing well back from the windows, hidden from view of the attackers, Sutter and Morgan scanned the surrounding country to see where the Indians might be concealed. There was only one possible place, which was a rise of ground with a little copse of trees at the summit. They couldn't see any sign of movement there, but for a bet that was the spot from which the arrows had been fired.

CHAPTER 9

What Little Feather and Horse-Born, with their extremely limited experience of firearms, quite failed to understand was that pistols are essentially close quarter weapons; quite different from rifles. The two of them were lying under the trees, looking down at the trading post and planning to shoot the men they had been tracking, as soon as they emerged from the house. At a distance of over a hundred yards, that would have been beyond the skill of even the most accomplished gunman, armed as they were with only .44 revolvers. Their opponents, on the other hand, were toting Winchesters which were well able to shoot accurately over a mere hundred yards.

Frobisher's wife was in the barn, bound and gagged and tied to a post. Little Feather and Horse-Born had not been too rough with her, although on discovering that she was not Cherokee but Choctaw, they had not been particularly gentle either. Now they were lying perfectly still and quiet beneath the trees, partly covered with last year's leaves. Without a good pair of field glasses, there would not have been the slightest chance of seeing them from the house.

Sutter and Morgan were old hands at this game. The one thing they were not about to do was go running out of the shelter of the house, possibly into a hail of gunfire. 'What d'you say,' said Sutter, 'one of us opens the window here and marks those trees, while one of us goes round back of the house and starts shooting?'

'Sure,' said Morgan. 'How'd you want to play it? You in here or me?'

'You're the better shot. Get that window open and then take aim at those trees.' Having said this, Sutter slipped out of the room, with a view to going out the front door of the house, which was on the opposite side from where they supposed their assailants to be hiding.

Jack Morgan was a cautious man by temperament, which initially saved his life that morning. As soon as Sutter had left the room, Morgan dropped to his hands and knees and crossed over to the window. Very carefully, doing his utmost to ensure that he did not allow anybody outside the house to catch a good sight of his body and thus make it the target for any arrows or bullets, Morgan began to inch up the casement. It was tedious and awkward work; opening a stiff sliding window in this way from the side, without standing squarely in front of it. For Morgan, though, this caution was well worth the time and trouble. He had seen men killed more than once, because they had lacked the patience for such rudimentary precautions.

Having succeeded in opening the window without exposing himself to danger, Morgan dropped to his hands and knees again and made his way to the corner of the room, where his rifle was propped. He picked it up and cocked the weapon, working a cartridge into the breach. Then, staying deep in the shadows of the room, he slowly rose to his feet and peered across the room and out of the window to the little copse of trees from which he and Sutter had supposed the arrows had come. The way the morning sun was slanting towards the trees, Morgan was sure that he could not be seen from the rise of ground, as long as he stayed well back from the window. Even so, he stood stock-still, just in case a glimpse of movement might alert those watching the house, that he was there.

While he was scanning the huddle of trees for any sign of life, Morgan tried to calculate the distance. He estimated that it was more than a hundred yards, but certainly less than two hundred. Looking down at the sights of the rifle, he decided to split the difference and call the range a hundred and fifty yards. His deft fingers adjusted the sights accordingly. Then he raised the Winchester to his shoulder and squinted down the barrel and watched for the first sign of movement.

It did not, thought Sutter, as he ran jinking from

side to side to the barn, take any genius to figure out that he and Morgan were under attack from Indians. Nor was it hard to work out that these were probably men who had been infuriated by Beauregarde shooting one of their number a little while back. Not for the first time, Jed Sutter mentally cursed the name, parentage and memory of the excitable little Creole. Even now that he was dead, Beauregarde was still causing problems!

It had been the work of a moment to dash up to the room where he and Morgan had slept and to bring down his own rifle. When he reached the barn, the first thing that Sutter saw was Frobisher's squaw; trussed up like a chicken and laying there in the dust. He went over and eased the length of cloth that was gagging her, over her head and away from her mouth.

'Who tied you up?' asked Sutter. 'Quick, now, there's no time to lose.'

'Two Cherokee,' replied the woman.

'They tell you what they're after?'

'White men.'

'That'd be me and my partner then, I dare say,' said Sutter, the ghost of a smile playing around his lips. 'They say anything else?'

The woman shook her head.

'Well,' said Sutter, 'I aim to kill those boys and I can do it a sight easier if there's no added difficulties, such as you hollering and screaming and most likely running round like a headless chicken into the bargain. So I'll be gagging you again, just for the duration of my fightin', you understand.'

'Crusher' Frobisher's wife made no protest, nor did she attempt to stop Sutter, when he pulled the cloth back up and tightened the knot in it, so that she was once again effectually gagged.

After making sure that the squaw wasn't about to interfere with his activities or get in the way by shouting a warning or anything of the sort, Sutter climbed the ladder leading to the hay-loft. He didn't trust Indians at all and wondered if the squaw was in some way mixed up in this affair. When he was in the loft, Sutter made his way to the wall facing the stand of trees from which he suspected the arrows had come. He guessed, quite correctly as it happened, that Frobisher himself must have built this barn. It was a dreadfully shoddy and slapdash piece of work with yawning gaps between the outer planks, so that the wind could howl through the place without the slightest let or hindrance. This poor workmanship worked now to Sutter's advantage, for it meant that he was able to gain a clear and unobstructed view out across to the trees in which he suspected the Indians were hiding.

At this point, neither Sutter nor Morgan had reason to suppose that the Indians were carrying firearms. They had been attacked with bows and arrows and, as far as they knew, that was the most deadly weapon that they would need to contend with. It was really only a question of staying low and then picking off the Indians as they showed themselves, perhaps by approaching closer to the house.

It was Horse-Born who precipitated the next stage of the fight. He had fired a scattergun belonging to his father on more than one occasion and felt that this made him some kind of expert as far as firearms were concerned. He had less patience than his companion and wanted to get things moving. He and Little Feather were lying beneath the trees, covered with a blanket of leaves which camouflaged them so well that you might have walked past them at a distance of six feet or so without even knowing that they were there. Very slowly, Horse-Born brought up the Remington and fired once at the house.

As soon as he saw the flash of fire, followed almost immediately by the puff of smoke and then the rolling report of the shot, Jack Morgan fired at once. His ball smacked into the bole of a tree near the two Indians. They then unleashed a perfect fusillade of fire at the house, not even considering for a moment that once they had each fired five shots; their pistols would be useless.

Over in the barn, Sutter waited quietly to see what the end result of all this gunfire would be. He would by no means be displeased if any harm befell Jack Morgan; he had not forgotten Morgan's sharp words to him and challenge to his leadership. Sutter was sure that, situated as he was up here, he would be well able to kill anybody who approached the house, before they came closer than fifty yards or so.

It was a one million to one, freak chance which ended Jack Morgan's never overly successful career as an outlaw. The revolvers being fired by the two young Cherokees up on the rise of ground nigh to the house were not accurate above a few yards. However, the killing power of a half ounce of lead was not diminished for some hundreds of yards, even if it was impossible at that distance to determine accurately where the bullet would end up. After that first shot from Horse-Born's pistol, to which Morgan had at once responded by firing back with his rifle, the two Indians had fired a further nine shots at the house, emptying the pistols in the process. One of these nine bullets found its mark.

Standing well back in the room, out of sight of anybody outside, Morgan felt completely safe. As far as it went, this was true; at least as far as the possibility of anybody being able to draw a bead on him went. What he did not factor in to his calculations was that a stray ball could still fly through that window, whether it was aimed or not. This is precisely what chanced with one of the nine shots fired by Horse-Born and Little Feather. One moment, Jack Morgan was standing there in the shadows, confident of his own safety, the next, he had dropped his rifle and clutched his hands to his face; where a .44 ball had blown out his left eye and entered his brain through the empty eye-socket. He dropped to his knees moaning in agony and very soon afterwards died from massive injury to his brain.

The sudden flurry of shooting greatly surprised Sutter. He would have taken oath that whoever was besieging the house was armed with nothing more dangerous than bows and arrows. His heart sank and he felt a chill feeling in his throat when the shooting began. However, after a few brief seconds, it all died down again and Sutter was able to take stock of the situation. The one thing he had not done was join battle on his own account. His hope was that those attacking the house would eventually be embold-ened and walk up to the door; at which point Sutter would be able to shoot them down from cover.

Sometimes, those with whom Sutter undertook robberies joked that he must have had Indian blood in him; he was that patient. On this occasion, he sat in the hay-loft for better than half an hour, waiting for the boys who had been firing to show themselves. Just as he had thought all along, they had been hiding up in that stand of trees and when he saw the two figures detach themselves from the leaves and grass, he fully expected Morgan to gun them down. That there was no shooting from the house, told Sutter at once that Jack Morgan was probably dead. Well, that was fine. He had been an uppity bastard, which nobody could deny, and he had been saved the trouble of killing the man himself by that morning's events.

Very cautiously, the two Indians stood up and then began walking down the slope towards the house and barn. Sutter waited until they were less than twenty yards from him and then he shot them both in quick succession. Once he had dropped them, Sutter fired twice at each of them where they lay, just to make quite sure that they were both dead. Then he stood up and stretched, before climbing down the ladder.

It has to be said that Jed Sutter was feeling pretty braced with things. He would need to check, but he was pretty sure that Morgan was now dead; which meant that all the money from that bank in Bluff Creek was now his. He had disposed of the two boys who had seemingly been intent on taking his life and to the best of his knowledge and belief, there was nobody else for him to worry about. He walked jauntily from the barn, into the bright sunshine; the Winchester held casually in one hand. Then, from close at hand and right behind him, he heard the unmistakable sharp, metallic click of a gun being cocked and somebody said, 'Don't you move a muscle, or you're as good as dead.'

Professor Carver and Runner had found each other to be comfortable travelling companions and the Indian obviously felt himself under orders from the dead Chief to do as Carver directed. As they tracked the party of robbers towards Frobisher's cantina, the professor's purpose hardened and became clearer to him; he would take the men back with him to Bluff Creek. How he would accomplish such a task, he had not the least notion, but he knew that he had to do it.

Since he had left Bluff Creek in hunt of the men

130

responsible for killing his parents, Carver had scarcely felt so much as a twinge of the guilt which had so overpowered him at first. He had an idea that if he could only bring them to justice by his own efforts, then he might be able to live with the regrets and shame that he still felt for the way that he had treated his mother and father. This expedition had worked on him just like a tonic in that respect; allowing him to forget the feelings which had so overwhelmed him when he had heard about the death of his family.

As they came closer to catching up with the three riders who they were tracking, Professor Carver had tried to get some idea of how far the man called Runner would be prepared to go in assisting him.

'Would you help me in capturing these men, if I asked?' said Carver at one point.

Runner turned his grave eyes upon the professor. 'Yes,' he said.

'You'd help me tie them up and so on?'

'I would do that.'

'Because the man who was once your Chief asked you to?'

'That is true.'

Professor Carver and his guide came to Frobisher's house just as the shooting began. As soon as he heard the first shot, Runner told Carver to dismount and secure his horse to a tree. At this point, they were not even in view of the cantina. By the time they were on the ground, there was another volley of shots; perhaps a dozen or so.

'There's a white man's place just ahead of us,' said Runner. 'That's where the shooting is, I think. If we walk round this way, we can end up right by the back of it and see what is happening.'

The two of them worked their way through the shrubbery and trees, until they were only a few yards from the barn. Runner gripped the professor's arm and signalled that he should just stand there without moving. Carver had brought the rifle with him and he held it half under his shoulder and ready to bring up to fire at the first sign of trouble.

From their vantage point, Professor Carver and his Indian guide could see only the barn, a small portion of the back of a stone built house and some of the open country beyond. Nothing was stirring and there was no sign of whoever had been doing the shooting. The two of them stood there for a space, without moving or speaking. Just when Carver was about to ask if it was safe to keep going, he noticed a movement in a little copse of trees about two hundred yards away. At first, he couldn't be sure whether he was seeing a couple of large animals like bears rearing to their hind legs, but when he looked a little closer, he realized that two men had got to their feet and were heading towards them.

The two young Indians who left the cover of the trees were gunned down before they came closer than fifty yards or so to Professor Carver's hiding place. The shots which killed them came from the right, which could only mean that the gunman was hiding in the barn. Runner indicated without speaking that they should now move forward and when they reached the barn door, he guided Carver to the wall of the barn and they stood there waiting. As a man emerged from the dark interior of the barn, Carver cocked his piece and said, 'Don't you move a muscle, or you're as good as dead.' Even as he spoke the words, they sounded absurd, like something you might see written in a dime novel.

Sutter knew at once that the man had the drop on him. He glanced back with an almost imperceptible turning of his head and saw that a tall white man had a rifle at his shoulder which was pointing straight at Sutter's back. He did not move any more, merely asking, 'What would you have me do?'

'Let drop that gun of yours. Just loosen your fingers and let the rifle fall from your grasp.'

Sutter obeyed instantly. Please God, there would be an opportunity later, when the odds were not stacked so high against him, but for now, there was little he could do other than to follow the instructions he was given. The man with the rifle said, 'Runner, can you relieve this gentleman of his guns? Don't cross my line of fire, though.'

Sutter was aware of being disarmed and did not at all take to the feeling of complete and utter helplessness engendered by the experience. He relished his predicament even less, when the man with the rifle trained on him said to his partner, 'Now bind his hands together in front of him, please.'

When the other man came into Sutter's field of vision, he was surprised to see that he was an Indian. He submitted meekly to being bound, it still wasn't the time yet for resistance. When he was more or less helpless, the man with the rifle moved round in front of him and said, 'What's your name?'

'Sutter. Jed Sutter.'

'Where are your friends?'

Sutter laughed shortly. 'I never was much of a one for friends,' he said, 'but such as I've had recently are all dead now.'

'Well, Mr Sutter, my friend and I have been following you for some little time. Would you care to guess why that might have been?'

'You want for to rob me?'

'No, that's not the case. I believe that you and some others robbed the bank in the town of Bluff Creek and murdered the sheriff there into the bargain.'

'Who says so?' asked Sutter, a look of surprised innocence upon his cunning face.

'That's nothing to the purpose,' said Professor Carver, looking closely at the man in front of him. 'Did you shoot those two men lying dead over there?'

Sutter shrugged, unwilling to commit himself.

At this point, to the professor's surprise, Runner took a hand in the conversation, saying, 'Those two men you killed were my friends. You shot them from ambush, like a coward.'

Leaving the man he had captured in the safekeeping of Runner, Carver checked the house and in doing so found the bodies of Frobisher and Morgan. It didn't take him long to find the proceeds of the bank robbery at Bluff Creek. Some of the bundles of bills even had the wrappers round them with the name of the bank stamped upon them. The professor went back to where Sutter was being guarded and said, 'I've seen enough to satisfy me that you are the man I have been looking for.'

Knowing as he did that the evidence to be found in his saddle-bag and that of his late friends was nigh on irrefutable, Sutter dropped his pose of injured innocence and said, 'Well, and what're you fixin' to do about it then?'

The mild-looking man said, 'I'm going to take you right back to Bluff Creek and see you answer for your crimes.'

'You'll find that a hard row to hoe.'

'We'll see.'

If Runner had not thought to look into the barn, it is altogether possible that Frobisher's wife might have stayed there, trussed up and gagged, until she died of starvation or thirst. Fortunately though, he did glance into the barn and as a consequence, the woman was freed and tended to until she had recovered somewhat from the ordeal which she had undergone.

It didn't take long for the Choctaw woman who had lived with Frobisher for so many years to sketch out the details of what had befallen her that morning. While she talked to Carver, Runner went off to see to the bodies of the two members of his clan who had been killed by Sutter. Although Runner had shown himself to be a quiet and sober sort of fellow, not given to shouting and violence, it was pretty plain to the professor that he was exceedingly displeased with Sutter for shooting down his friends from cover in that way. Carver wondered if the man who had acted as his guide would still be so agreeable to his taking Sutter back to Bluff Creek to answer for his crimes there, or whether he was planning to settle with the outlaw here and now.

While Professor Carver spoke to Frobisher's wife, Jed Sutter glowered in the background, obviously seething at being tied up and taken prisoner. Although he had little experience of such things, it seemed to Carver that this was a dangerous man and that getting him to Bluff Creek might be no easy task.

When Runner came back from his examination of Horse-Born and Little Feather's bodies, he walked casually up to where Sutter was standing and then landed a tremendous backhanded blow across the man's face. It was delivered with lip-bursting force and blood at once began to run down Sutter's chin from his nose and mouth. The professor watched, horrified, as this happened, confidently expecting that Runner would next take out his knife and plunge it into the outlaw's heart. Instead, the Indian turned away from Sutter and said to Professor Carver,

'I am sorry. He is a cowardly assassin and I had to let him know how I feel.'

'Yes, I feel much the same way about him,' said Carver. 'All the same, I have it in mind to take him back to Bluff Creek. You don't plan to kill him, I suppose?'

'I gave a promise,' said Runner, 'and I would not break my word. He is lucky that I did. Otherwise, he would be dead now.'

CHAPTER 10

It took a couple of hours to sort through the carnage in and around Frobisher's cantina. Professor Carver invited the dead man's widow to accompany either him or Runner when they left, but she expressed the wish to remain there in the house. Whatever she planned to do, she didn't choose to share it with them.

In addition to the large amount of cash money stashed in it, Sutter's saddle-bag contained a most astonishing document. It was a letter addressed to Sutter and when the professor read it, his eyes widened in shock. This, he tucked carefully into the inside pocket of his jacket. After having gathered together all the proceeds of the robbery and placed them on his own horse, Carver was ready to leave. He did not wish to take the long road back to Bluff Creek and was particularly anxious to avoid passing nearby to the settlement where the dead Cherokees had lived. He consulted with Runner about this.

'I can point you on a straighter road than that we came here by,' said Runner. 'You need not travel east and north and then east again to reach your town. We had to track this man along his crooked path, but going back, you can take a direct road.'

'You're not coming with me?' asked Carver.

The young Cherokee shook his head. 'I must burn the bodies of my brothers. I cannot leave the woman here alone. She is Choctaw and they are no friends of ours, but even so, I must take her back to her own people.'

Such solicitude for a member of an enemy tribe struck Professor Carver as something quite wonderful, especially as so many people viewed Indians as being little better than savages. He said, 'You have the soul of an old-time knight. You will not break an oath and you wish to protect a lady, even if she is nothing to do with you. Your conduct does you credit.'

For the first time since he had met Runner, a faint smile appeared on the man's lips and he said, 'Like King Arthur and his knights, you mean?'

Carver was staggered, for that was precisely what he had been hinting at. He said, 'I have underestimated you and I apologize. Yes that is exactly what I meant, but I didn't expect—'

This time, Runner's smile was open. He said, 'Didn't expect a red Indian to have heard of the Knights of the Round Table? You forget, I grew up with white missioners. These were the tales they told us after our lessons were over.'

Standing nearby, his hands bound in front of him with rawhide thongs, Jed Sutter said, 'You men goin' to talk about a lot of foolishness or are we to ride out? You sound like women, the way you chatter.'

'I wonder that you're in any great hurry,' Carver remarked, 'seeing that the end of this expedition is likely to see you hanging from a rope. Still and all, if you are that eager to meet your death, then we had best start out. The afternoon's passing.'

So it was that Professor Carver and his prisoner rode north, along a road which would, according to Runner, bring them to Bluff Creek in no more than forty-eight hours.

Sutter was not a talkative man, which suited the professor well enough. He had plenty of thinking to do. What was perfectly clear to him was that under-taking this journey was the best thing that he could possibly have done. He had known for the last few years that he had treated his parents in the most shabby way imaginable and although there was nothing which could be done about that, he hoped that he had made some sort of amends by tracking down and capturing one of their killers. If nothing else, it had served to take his mind off his guilt in the days following their deaths.

The possibility was ever-present in Carver's mind that the man riding with him might at some stage attempt to escape. For this reason, he was deter-mined that no matter how inconvenient for his

140

prisoner, he would not be untying Sutter's hands for the duration of their trip together. He also insisted that his captive rode ahead of him, so that he could keep an eye on him. Sutter was a hard one to read, but it wasn't hard to guess that he thought Professor Carver unlikely to be up to the job of taking him all the way back to Bluff Creek to answer for his crimes. Carver prided himself on being a pretty good judge of character and his estimation of this man's temperament and disposition was that he was as mean and dangerous as a rattlesnake.

That first night, the two of them camped by a stream. Carver had brought enough rations to keep them from hunger for a two-day trip, but the fare was by no means luxurious. There was bread, cheese, slices of cold meat and coffee. After they had eaten, Sutter still in a sullen and uncommunicative frame of mind, the professor said to him, 'Well, Mr Sutter, I suppose that we should discuss our arrangements for the night.'

The other man looked up curiously and said, 'Yeah, I'd like to hear what you propose.'

'It's simple enough. You're going to sit with your back to a tree and I'm going to secure you to it with rope.'

'Say I don't agree to sit so?'

'Then I'll shoot you. Oh, I won't kill you, but I guarantee I'll cause a bad injury. Maybe shatter your wrist or something of the sort. What do you say, are you going to make this hard for yourself?'

Sutter shot him a look of pure hatred, but when the time came for them to settle down for the night, he did not put up any opposition to the arrangement that Professor Carver had outlined. Carver secured the rope to the thong binding Sutter's wrists and then wound it around the tree, so that the knots were all on the other side of the trunk. Despite these precautions, Carver still chose to sleep some good distance from the tree to which his prisoner was tied.

It was not a pleasant and relaxed night and Professor Carver felt pretty dreadful in the morning. Despite having spent the last few nights sleeping rough, out in the open, he didn't really take to the scheme. Carver was aware that there were men, his own father had been one such, to whom sleeping out of doors like this was a rare treat. Apart from the rank discomfort of lying upon the stony ground, rather than a soft mattress, there had been throughout the whole night, the constant apprehension that Jed Sutter would somehow find a way to free himself and then launch a murderous attack upon him.

All in all, Carver was pleased and relieved when dawn came. He built a small fire of pine cones and twigs and then endeavoured to boil up some coffee. It looked to him as though Sutter had not spent a night any more relaxed and comfortable than his own. 'You want some coffee?' he asked Sutter.

'I feel like shit.'

'That makes two of us, but that wasn't what I asked. I offered you some coffee.'

142

After carefully freeing Sutter from the tree, Carver placed a tin cup of coffee on the ground for the man to pick up. He himself retreated a safe distance and covered the outlaw with his rifle. He wasn't about to have a cup of scalding hot liquid dashed in his face as part of an escape bid.

'They say the Choctaw are on the warpath,' observed Sutter, in a conversational tone of voice. 'You hear 'bout that?'

'Can't say that I did,' replied Professor Carver, 'but it makes no difference to our plans.'

'Why, man, how can you say so? Ain't we heading right into the Choctaw Nation this very day?'

'If we are, then we'll be leaving it by tonight,' said Carver imperturbably. 'I'm not going to change our route because of some rumour.'

'Don't say as I didn't warn you.'

'I promise that I shall make no such suggestion.'

It was a beautiful day and Carver, who generally preferred books to nature any day of the week, could not help but find his heart lifted by the sun and the fluffy white clouds scudding along through the azure sky. He was minded to remark upon this to the man with whom he was travelling, but some natural delicacy prevented him. After all, this Sutter might not have much longer to enjoy this world. It would perhaps be tactless and crass to tell him how wonderful it all looked.

The first intimation that they might be in some hazard came at a little after midday. They had been riding at a steady trot since breaking camp an hour or so after sunup and were making good time. The country through which the two men were passing was flat, with rocky bluffs rising at irregular intervals. The road or track along which they were travelling wove its way between these stony outcrops. As they were riding across an especially flat area, Sutter said in a neutral and unconcerned way, 'There's a body o' horsemen trailin' us away over yonder to the left.'

Professor Carver reined in his horse, which irritated Sutter no end. He too stopped, but said, 'You're a damned fool if you think this is a time to halt. Like as not they're hostile. We need to go faster, not stop here and wait for 'em to kill us.'

'Who do you think they are? Friends of yours?'

'Not hardly. I'd lay odds they're Choctaw warriors.'

'We'll canter for a spell, then. Don't forget though, I'm right behind you with a rifle near at hand. Any sign of your fleeing and I promise you I'll shoot.'

The two of them rode on for a half hour and at the end of that time, it was fairly plain that the half dozen or so men riding parallel to them were closing in and, even more alarming, were overtaking them; presumably with the aim of cutting ahead of them. Carver called to Jed Sutter, 'This won't answer. They'll be upon us in another fifteen minutes.'

Sutter slowed his horse right down and said, 'Give me your rifle. I'll warrant I'm a better shot than you. If I have the rifle and you keep that pistol, we'll do well enough between the two of us.'

'It's not to be thought of,' said Carver shortly. 'You'd kill me and then bolt for it. I know what brand you are, Sutter, for all that I've not had much experience of men like you.'

'Well then, what do you want? We wait here for them until they come and kill us?'

In the farthest reaches of Joseph Carver's mind, the first glimmerings of an idea were beginning to take shape. He said slowly, 'No, I don't think we should sit here and wait for them. I say we ought to make for that bluff across there.'

Sutter looked in the direction that the professor was pointing and said, 'That's a good six or seven miles away. We'll never make it.'

'Let's try.'

So the two men, the university professor and the ruthless outlaw, turned their horses and began first trotting and then cantering towards a rocky eminence which towered above the otherwise flat land. They were, as Sutter had predicted, unable to gain the bluff before the party of riders cut ahead of them. Carver knew little about Indians and was wholly unable to distinguish one tribe or racial group from another, but it seemed to him that, judging by their behaviour alone, they were very angry and probably meant mischief to him and his companion.

Professor Carver and Sutter reined in when they were about fifty yards from the seven men ahead of them. There was a tense moment when it looked uncertain what would next happen and then an arrow came sailing through the air towards them. It fell short, but Carver didn't wish to take any chances. He unslung his rifle and fired at the men, who promptly took flight. They didn't go far, though. They evidently didn't have any firearms of their own and were keeping their distance for now. Once Carver and Sutter started off again, the seven Indians followed them, keeping far enough away that it would not be easy to pick them off with a rifle.

It wasn't necessary, thought Professor Carver to himself, to be any great military tactician to work out what would happen next. These men would tail them until night fell and then move in for the kill under circumstances in which the white man's weapons would not profit him. He was a poor enough shot in broad daylight; his chances of picking off every one of a group of attacking Indians in the pitch dark were negligible.

'You got any sort of a plan?' said Sutter, 'cause I can tell you for now, those devils have a sight more patience than any white men. They'll follow us until we sleep or rest and then kill the both of us.'

'I have a plan. It hinges upon our being able to reach that rocky escarpment.'

'That what?' said Sutter. 'Why'nt you try talkin' like a normal man?'

'Is it your impression, Mr Sutter, that those men are starting to crowd us again?'

'Yeah, you might say so.'

146

'That was my idea, also.' Carver took the rifle from his back, worked a cartridge into the breach and then fired once more in the general direction of the Indians, who then rode hard to get further out of range. But they were still riding parallel to the professor and his captive and clearly had no present intention of backing off and leaving them be.

By now, they were only a mile from the limestone crags that formed the nearest bluff. Carver could see that the cliffs, which at first sight appeared sheer and impenetrable, were in fact split with fissures and gullies; wide enough, or so it seemed to him, for riders to pass through. Ahead of him, Sutter said, 'You want that we should make for that nearest gap in the rocks?'

'That's right,' said Professor Carver, hoping that his idea was a sound one. Whether or no, it was the only one that he had. The Indians were holding back, to see what their quarry would do next.

When the two men reached the cliffs, they found themselves facing a cleft, which was perhaps ten or twelve feet wide. This was in effect a gorge in the limestone formation, big enough for Professor Carver and Jed Sutter to ride their horses through. On either side, the rock rose sheer and smooth. As they rode into this gloomy little chasm, Carver said, 'How quickly are you able to mount your horse and start riding?'

Sutter looked puzzled. 'I'm already on my horse,' he said. 'What are you talkin' about?'

147

'We're going to dismount shortly,' replied Carver, 'and then we're going to jump back on our horses and race for our lives.'

'You think now's the time to get down from our mounts?'

'I'm convinced of it. Dismount right now or we'll both die right here.'

It isn't as easy to get down from a horse when your wrists are lashed together, but Sutter managed it and stood there, wondering if this was where he had a chance to lamp this well-spoken bastard and hightail it out of there. It was apparently not the right time, for Carver said to him, 'Sit over there, facing away from me.'

Once the outlaw was seated on the ground and couldn't see what he was up to, Professor Carver took his rifle and loped to the entrance to the cleft, along which he and the other man were about to travel. Just as he had suspected would be the case, the pursuing Indians had speeded up and were now, by the look of them, about to ride after them into the gap between the cliffs. The professor fired a shot at them, whereupon the seven riders turned and fled, regrouping a little further off. Without delay, Carver ran back to his horse and delved into the saddle-bag, extracting a small, wooden cask, wound round with what appeared to be a length of string.

Sutter turned round and said, 'What in the hell are you up to?'

'Never you mind. Just be ready to vault on to that

horse of yours, just as soon as I give the word.'

Two things struck Sutter most powerfully. The first was that for all that he spoke in that fancy way, wore eyeglasses and was very obviously unused to rough living; this was a man who was capable of handling a tricky situation very neatly and without any fuss. Even his insistence on having Sutter dismount and sit facing away from him, showed that he knew how to arrange things well for his own ends. The other thing which stood out was that here was somebody enjoying himself. Even Sutter was beginning to get a little jittery and beginning to fear that they would fall into the hands of the Choctaw and be slowly tortured to death. This man, though, was having a good time. It was fascinating to observe.

These reflections were interrupted when the professor suddenly cried to Sutter, 'Come on, get on your horse. We have to leave right now.'

Even then, there was no opportunity to turn the tables on the son of a bitch. He was still covering Sutter casually with his rifle. At first, Sutter was disposed to play for time and see if he could find an opening for an attack. It was then that he glimpsed a shower of sparks coming from behind a pile of rocks and heard a faint hissing and sputtering.

'Hey, what is that?' he asked curiously.

'It's five pounds of fine-grain black powder, with a fuse on it that's already burning,' Professor Carver told him calmly.

Sutter let out what would, in any less brave and

manly character, have been described as a yelp of
fear and cried, 'God almighty, have you taken leave
of your senses? We got to get out o' here!'

'That,' said Carver, moving towards his own horse,
'is why I said we had to leave.'

Jed Sutter fairly ran to his mount and was in the
saddle and away in a matter of seconds. Professor
Carver followed him. It was not possible to get the
horses to travel very fast over the limestone floor of
the gully. The rock was slick and the last thing either
of them wanted was to end up laming their horses.

When they had gone about fifty yards, Sutter
glanced back and saw the Choctaw entering the gap
in the cliffs. He said to Carver, 'How long was that
fuse?'

'I don't rightly know. I reckon that it should reach
the powder any second now.'

At that very moment, there was a noise like a crack
of thunder which was directly overhead. The stone
walls of the gorge magnified the sound and left their
ears ringing. The horses were terrified; rearing up
and whinnying in shock, their eyes widening in fear.
It was all that Sutter and the professor could do to
bring them back under control.

From the direction that they had come, a roiling
black cloud billowed towards them and in the eerie
silence, they could hear little stones and bits of grit
showering down on to the rocky floor of the gully.
Even now, Carver kept a weather eye on his prisoner,
but the other man seemed too taken aback to be

thinking of escape. He looked genuinely overawed by the explosion which had shaken the bluff.

As the smoke cleared, it revealed a scene of horror. The cliff faces between which the Choctaw had been riding had concentrated the force of the blast, reflecting it back upon itself. The effects upon those seven horses and riders had thus been increased many-fold. Even from where they were, they could see the blood, which was splashed liberally up the rocky walls of the gully and the fragments of horses and their riders, which were scattered far and wide. There did not look to be any survivors.

'I never seen anything like it in my life,' said Sutter. 'You killed every last one of them.'

Carver shrugged. 'They would have killed us.' He raised his rifle and said to Sutter, 'We're riding back the way we came. You go first. And don't think about trying to make a run. You know I'd fire.'

The entrance to the little gully was quite literally awash with gore. In the narrow confines of the gorge, the charge had blown their pursuers to pieces and allowed each one of them to pour out his life's blood on the limestone floor. Sutter and the professor had to slow their mounts down to a walk as they picked their way across the pools of blood. It was a relief to get out of the shadowy space and back into the fresh air and sunshine.

By nightfall, they had reached the line separating Kansas from the Indian Territories. There was no border or anything of that sort; it was rather that the land became progressively more cultivated and less wild. The two men hadn't talked much after the massacre at the bluff. Professor Carver was not proud of his actions, however necessary they had been and as for Sutter, he had been awed by the casual way that the man who had taken him prisoner had disposed of seven living men.

They camped out again; Carver once more tying his prisoner to a tree. He was slightly apologetic about it, saying, 'I mind this isn't the most comfortable way to spend the night, but we should be back in Bluff Creek by tomorrow afternoon. I dare say they'll give you a proper bed for the night there.' Sutter shot him a sour look.

CHAPTER 11

The weather was marvellous and Professor Carver couldn't recollect when last he had so enjoyed a trip through the countryside. In the general way of things, his life was centred around towns and he never caught more than a fleeting glimpse of fields and trees from the window of some railroad car. As the two of them headed north east towards Bluff Creek, Carver found his mind turning to some of the expeditions that he had been on with his father, when he was much younger. Only, he thought, in those days he wasn't my 'father'; he was just plain 'Pa'.

There was something a little melancholy about these reflections and he looked over to Sutter, to see if the man was in the mood for talking. The professor could have done with taking out of himself a little. Sutter, though, looked to be sunk in a brown study. Considering that the fellow was probably facing the hangman's rope in a few weeks, Carver couldn't find it in his heart to blame the man for being a little thoughtful.

'I'm sorry,' said Carver, 'that you're left to carry the can for this alone, as one might say. I know there was a group of you and I make no doubt that you were all equally guilty.'

'You're sure of that, are you?' asked Sutter, with a sneer. 'How so?'

'Because I heard that there was a regular gang of you men robbing the bank and that my father was shot by one of you. Still, it is what the law calls a "joint enterprise" and what one does, then all must answer for. I suppose you knew when you set out that robbing that bank was unlawful?'

'I tell you one thing, you long-winded son of a bitch,' said Sutter, 'I'll be right glad in a manner o' speakin' to be locked up in the gaol-house. Least the men there are apt to talk like normal men, without a lot of ten-dollar words.' Those were the last words that they exchanged before reaching Bluff Creek.

The reappearance of Will Carver's boy, as the older inhabitants of the town thought of him, caused a minor sensation in the town. There had been those who thought it right coldhearted of Joseph Carver to go skipping off like that as soon as his ma and pa were in the ground. Now, as he rode down Main Street with a man whose hands were tied together like a prisoner, there was the liveliest speculation as to what the story was behind it all.

Dave Starr and Bob Watkins were both in the

sheriff's office and when Will Carver's son fetched up there with a prisoner, both men looked astounded, as well they might. 'What's going on, Mr Carver?' asked Watkins. 'Who's this?'

'This is the man, or at least one of the men, who robbed the bank and shot my father,' Professor Carver informed him calmly. 'I'm delivering him into your custody. Take care of him, now, he's a dangerous one.'

'Begging your pardon, sir,' said Watkins, 'but do you have any evidence or aught of the kind? Something to show his connection with the crime? Not as I doubt your word, you understand, but I need to know what's what.'

'If you'll set a watch upon this fellow, then I'll bring in from my horse as much evidence as you could hope for. Don't let him loose, mind, until I return.'

There was something so calm and authoritative about the way that their boss's son spoke, that both deputies were slightly overawed. 'Sure thing,' said Dave Starr. 'We'll keep him safe.'

Afterwards, Carver knew that he should have shown his hand at once, but he had always been one for dotting all the 'I's and crossing the 'T's. This was well enough in the academic world, but it wasn't really the best strategy here, because no sooner had he walked back out into the street, than he heard shouting and a commotion behind him, followed quickly by the sound of a single shot. He drew his pistol and turned back into the office.

Bob Watkins lay on the floor, and Dave Starr stood looking down at him, a look of almost comical dismay on his unintelligent face. As Sutter turned towards the professor, the gun that he had snatched from Watkins' holster still gripped in his hand, Professor Carver shot him without a moment's hesitation. Then he pointed his gun at Dave Starr and said, 'You'll answer for this business.'

'I swear I didn't know what he was about to do,' cried Starr fearfully. 'He just went forward so fast; I couldn't o' stopped him if I tried.'

'You are a terrible liar, Mr Starr,' said Professor Carver, not angrily but in a conversational way. 'Tell me, what relation was Sutter to you? A relative, old friend?'

Seeing that his hand was now turned over and proved to have no winning cards in it, Starr said resignedly, 'He was my cousin.'

'You should not have written to him, you know. At least, not using your real name.'

'I never meant your pa to come to harm. I thought he'd o' finished work right early that day. Jeez, it was the last day of his working life. How could I've guessed that he'd still be patrolling the streets an hour before he retired?'

'You didn't know him very well,' said the professor, 'if you thought my pa was a man to take a day's pay and not give a day's work in exchange for it.' My pa, thought Carver, even as he spoke. Yes, I guess that he

156

was my pa. It sounded more natural and fitting somehow than to talk of his 'father'.

Professor Carver took out the crumpled and semi-literate letter which he had found after the shootout at the Frobisher place. Still keeping a wary eye upon Dave Starr, he read out loud, 'The old man is quitting on the 4th and you may be sure he won't be around in the afternoon. I'll lead the other man off on some snipe hunt. . . .' Carver shook his head sadly. 'You even signed it, "Dave". You surely are not cut out for a life of crime.'

'Your pa, he was after giving the job of sheriff to somebody else, after all the help we give him, me and Bob. Said I wasn't sharp enough to make a sheriff.'

'He got that right.'

It took a few days to clear things up in Bluff Creek and explain the ins and outs of the affair to the town council and other citizens who mattered. It was rightly judged that Dave Starr, although he might have provided the information which led to the bank being robbed, had no intention of causing the death of Will Carver. Like as not, he would draw a sentence of a couple of years in the penitentiary for his role in the business.

Now, in a novel, Joseph Carver would have decided that he really was his father's son and had a bent for law enforcement. He would have given up his post at the university and moved into his parents' old house and become sheriff of Bluff Creek. As a matter of fact, there *was* some talk of this kind by those who had known him as a boy. There were few people in town who had not been immensely impressed at the way that Will Carver's boy had set out alone and brought the killer of his mother and father to justice. It was felt that it might have been fitting to have appointed him sheriff in place of his father. Whether Professor Carver caught wind of these tentative plans or not, he stayed around only long enough to see Dave Starr taken off in irons, before arranging the sale of his childhood home and booking a passage back to his staid and respectable life in academia.

Before leaving town for what he thought would probably be the last time, the professor took a turn up and down Main Street. He did not think it at all likely that he would ever be returning to Bluff Creek and so wanted to take a last look at the place.

The guilt that Carver had felt about rejecting his parents and their background so comprehensively over the years had largely been eradicated by his actions over the last week or so. That being so, he felt that he might now be able to view the town in which he had grown up with a slightly less jaundiced and more objective eye. It didn't work, though. Bluff Creek still epitomized everything that he loathed and despised about small towns and their ways. The old buildings which he recalled from his childhood were not a whit less irritating now, than they had been on all his previous visits to the town following